HER DAUGHTER'S LIES

An addictive and unputdownable
psychological thriller with a killer twist
Mikayla Davids

To all the readers who've been so supportive: thank you, it means the world.

Contents

Prologue

She's not breathing.

Not again. Please, not again. We've already buried enough bodies.

The thought screams inside my head as I stare at the limp figure lying on the grass, her dirty hair spread around her pale, beautiful face. The paramedic bends over her, trying to find a pulse, and another thought hurtles into my brain: *I can't lose yet another member of my family.* I've endured too many losses; I don't think I can take another.

As the paramedics begin to start CPR on her too-still chest, the events of this evening's party come flooding back to me. Happy conversations by the bar, joyful embraces with distant relatives and scores of people drinking and enjoying themselves on the dance floor.

I should have known it was all about to go horribly wrong.

I shiver, the cold night air cutting through the thin fabric of my dress. There have always been too many lies in my family; too many people hiding the truth from one another. I'd hoped the past was finally behind us.

But the secrets revealed tonight have turned our lives upside down once again. And more than one person has too much to lose if the truth goes beyond our family circle.

I turn away, guttural sobs beginning to rise in my throat. I can't bear to watch as the paramedic tries to breathe life back into one of the people I love most in this world. I blink back the tears that threaten to fall.

Striding through the damp grass, I try to put some distance between myself and the desperate scene behind me. I replay snippets of the events of the evening: the music, my daughter's voice and the sound of the ambulance siren blur together in my mind. I'm still in shock.

It was supposed to be an evening of laughter and celebration. The perfect night. How did it come to this?

I know the answer. My daughter's lies have led us here. Because of her, I may soon be burying another member of the Bailey family...

Chapter One
Nadia

Standing in front of the beautiful old building, I take a deep breath and steady my nerves. It's a bright summer afternoon and the red-brick English country mansion set against the blue sky looks picturesque. Burcott House is a five-star boutique hotel, complete with lavender fields and golf course. People book up months in advance to stay here. And it's the type of property that people would kill to own.

There should be nothing unnerving about it at all. But, despite how popular the hotel is, it's the one place in the world that I hate coming to. The ivy curled around the pretty sash windows makes my stomach drop. I've woken up repeatedly in the dead of night, panting for breath, after distorted images of this ivy have slithered their way into my darkest dreams, twisting and turning like tentacles.

Because behind the building's pretty exterior lies a dark history. Nearly a decade ago, Burcott House was a murder scene. The image of a dead body splayed across the white, marble floor is something you can't forget easily. Or at least I can't.

As I hurry along the wide pathway, my feet crunching on the gravel, I force myself to put one foot in front of the other. I don't want to be here but I have no choice. The nightmare that began almost a decade ago isn't quite over. The last few years have been uneventful – almost normal – and I've tricked myself into pretending this day wouldn't come. But as I run my fingers through my short, spiky blonde hair I know the time has finally arrived for me to deal with my family's complicated past...

The front door is already open and a light breeze is filtering into the reception area of the recently renovated hotel. I make my way into the building, catching the smell of an expensive reed diffuser – a hint of orange and something else. I try to focus on the scent as I pass the winding staircase that I will forever associate with the terrible crime I witnessed.

I push open a heavy oak door, which swings shut behind me, and step into a pitch-black room. It's the middle of the day, so why is the room in darkness? Turning towards the wall, I fumble for the light switch and, when I finally manage to locate it, the room is filled with blinding light.

Closing my eyes and slowly reopening them, I allow my eyesight to readjust. I get goosepimples all over my body along with the sensation that I am not alone. Then someone behind me coughs.

Whirling around, I gasp out loud, unable to believe what I'm seeing. My hands fly to my mouth in shock as I take in the enormous, central room of the hotel which is filled with smiling faces. The thick curtains are closed tight and the overhead lights still feel too bright.

'What's going on?' I manage to squeak but my question goes unheard as I'm drowned out by a loud chorus of: 'Surprise!'

There must be at least seventy people in the room, if not more. I register a number of my family and friends. My eyes flit between them, I'm searching for one person in particular, but the faces swim in front of me as tears spring to my eyes. I can't focus properly to take it all in. Everyone has burst into a round of applause and a few people are cheering. I'm completely stunned and I don't know what to do with myself.

'Grandma!' My eighteen-year-old granddaughter Freya appears before me, giving me a quick hug before taking both of my hands in hers. 'You really had no idea, did you?'

My reaction answers her question and she laughs in delight. 'Come on!' she insists, dragging me towards the small stage on the opposite side of the room. I allow her to propel me through the body of people in the room and, as we go, I catch glimpses of grinning friends wearing smart suits and shiny dresses. I look down at my own faded jeans and loose-fitting top and wish I'd put on my light maxi dress this morning instead.

'Here we are.' Freya beams as she pushes me centre stage.

I stumble over my own feet, and for one awful moment, I think I'm going to fall. Now that I'm retired, I'm probably more active than when I was working. I go to my local gym at least twice a week and spend hours on end gardening but even still my balance is not what it once was. A hand steadies me and I look gratefully to my left, expecting it to be Freya but instead find myself confronted by another face that looks so similar to Freya's and yet so different.

My other granddaughter, Ophelia, has the same flame-coloured hair and the same heart-shaped face. Even though they're cousins, not sisters, Ophelia and Freya are regularly mistaken for twins. Ophelia is wearing a pink, shimmery, floor-length dress and her make-up is perfectly matched whereas Freya is make-up free and she's wearing a more under-stated aquamarine summer dress with spaghetti straps, her hair in loose waves.

Not for the first time, I wonder how my girls have grown up so quickly. Ophelia reaches for my hand, and I note her nail varnish is also precisely coordinated with the rest of her outfit. She's wearing a white sash with *Birthday Girl* embossed across it. She slips a matching sash over my own head and beams before turning us to face the rest of the room.

Ophelia's birthday is close to my own and she turns eighteen next week. I can tell that Ophelia is loving the attention as everyone begins to sing 'Happy Birthday' to both of us. My own response is quite the opposite. Heat rises in my cheeks; I'm embarrassed to have such a fuss made of me and I'm feeling more than a little self-conscious as I stand here in my old gardening clothes. I'd come here today to meet Ophelia for a coffee and a catch up. I wasn't expecting all of this. I'm definitely not dressed for such an occasion and I'm already thinking about how to extract myself so I can go and smooth my hair and add some blusher and mascara to my face.

Taking in the foil balloons and bunting along with a floral arch display over the door leading into the gardens, it's clear someone has gone to a lot of trouble to set this up. Freya is looking up at me, her green eyes shining with happiness – and on either side of her are two of my daughters. Sasha, my eldest, is moving her lips in sync with the lyrics but I can tell she isn't singing properly. I also can't help noticing that she has a deep crease etched between her eyebrows. Leah, my youngest daughter, is smiling widely but her eyes look puffy and tired, like she's been crying.

I could be reading too much into things but a mother can always tell when there's something wrong with her children. Maybe organising this joint birthday celebration has been stressful? I try to convince myself this must be the explanation, rather than letting my thoughts turn to more worrying alternatives.

'Happy birthday!' the crowd bellows, snapping me out of my thoughts as they come to the end of their very tuneless and uncoordinated version of the happy birthday song.

Scanning the sea of people in front of me, I think about the one person who should be here who isn't: Erin. My middle daughter was lost in a snowstorm in the French Alps, not long after the murder that took place at this hotel. There's been no trace of Erin ever since – she's never been found. What happened on the night of her disappearance still weighs heavily on me. As a family, we've been left in limbo, unsure whether to grieve or to hope that she's survived. I think about her every day.

Then everyone raises their glasses to toast Ophelia and I. I should be enjoying the evening but I'm on edge and can't relax. I take a sip of my champagne, the bubbles dancing on my tongue. I can't help wondering who organised this surprise party. Was it Sasha and Leah?

Because I didn't come back to Burcott House to drink champagne and dance. Today isn't significant just because of this party and the birthday celebrations for my granddaughter and I. This date has been lodged in my mind for several weeks. I have come back to Burcott House under the guise of meeting Ophelia but actually I had an ulterior motive.

After endless heartache, I planned to bury the past once and for all tonight. There's one more thing that I need to take care of, to ensure that my family is kept safe. Did somebody know that? Did someone unravel my plans and set this party up as a trap? Or am I just being paranoid?

I hope it's just a coincidence the party has fallen on today of all days. The hairs on the back of my neck stand on end as I consider the alternative. If anyone suspects the truth, then my precious family might be in greater danger than I'd realised...

Chapter Two

Ophelia

'Ophelia – *darling* – look at you. You look so much like your mother. That dress is divine! A total vision!' A family friend air kisses me and goes on and on about the design of my dress and how tall I am. I almost roll my eyes.

'I'm sure Erin would've been very proud of the person you're becoming. She would've just loved tonight – it's such a shame she's not here...'

I bite down hard on my tongue. Could she be any more insensitive? Doesn't this woman realise how much therapy I've had? Or how much work I've put in to try and get over the loss of my mum? Doesn't she have a filter?

'I'm sure the police could've done more to try and find her. Poor thing. It's too late now, I don't expect they'll ever discover the truth. A mystery...'

People have no clue. I want to slap her hard across the face. The worst thing is I'm going to have to go through a repeat of this again and again tonight. I should be used to it by now. But how do you ever get used to the fact that your mum has been missing for years? You don't get to say goodbye. There's just an endless question stretching across everything you do.

'Thank you, thank you,' I say through a fake smile, before pretending that I need to go to the bathroom. I don't care if she thinks I'm being rude. I just need a few minutes to myself. I still find it hard when people speculate about my mum like this. I head out of the Winchester Room and down the hallway that leads to the front of the hotel.

Pausing by a mirror, I rearrange my hair, and dab on some lip gloss. The older I get, the more I can see my mum staring back at me when I look at my reflection. I have the same bow-shaped lips, the same nose smattered with freckles. I'm even the same height she was. But it's me in the mirror, not her.

Everyone always comments on this, they tell me I'm the spitting image of my mum with my long copper-coloured hair and bright green eyes. They say that I even sound like her. I know for some people that's hard but I'm glad that I look like her because I don't want my mum to be forgotten. But I wish people would talk about my mum as a person instead of just obsessing over what they think happened to her. I just want to remember all the things I loved about her, like how smart she was and how wide her smile was. But no-one seems to be as keen to talk about those things.

I would do anything for my mum to be here today – to be celebrating my eighteenth birthday party. She's been missing from every family gathering, every celebration photo, every parents' evening. There isn't a day that goes by when I don't desperately want to see her.

Suddenly, I'm at the spot by the winding staircase where my dad died on the cold marble floor. Hardly anyone mentions him or talks about how his life ended so violently. I guess my aunts and my grandmother didn't really know him that well. And my dad's family are still reeling from the damage his murder caused to their name. The Scotts are incredibly wealthy and well-connected so their reputation is very important to them. My grandfather Hugo has maintained a silence around Dad's death and a stiff British upper lip that shows no sign of wobbling.

Sighing, I mentally preparing myself to face people again. I've learnt to be a good actress because when I come across as confident and bubbly, then I'm given some breathing space. If I don't walk around with a smile on my face then I end up with teachers or family members suggesting I need to go back to the doctors and re-evaluate my medication. It's just easier to pretend that everything is OK. It's how I got through the majority of my teenage years.

Hanging on one of the walls in the hallway is a portrait of me that was done not long before my life changed dramatically. I'm completely different to the little girl in the painting. Being orphaned when I was nine was tough, but it taught me to be even tougher. It's shaped every part of my life. But I'm about to turn eighteen and I'm ready for my family to stop treating me like a child. I'm ready to create my own life. I want to carve my own way in the world and I've got big ideas on how I might do that. Except there are things I need to understand about my past before I can get on with my future.

I'm sick of my family skirting around what really happened to my mum and dad. I'm sick of the vague half-truths; the mess of the past has been brushed under an expensive rug and hidden away. It drives me mad. My brother Jasper is OK with this; he doesn't want or need to know the truth.

But I do.

And I'm going to find out.

Chapter Three

Nadia

As my head spins and the world around me tilts on its axis, I stand still and try to calm myself. The noise levels increase as the partygoers chat to each other and music begins to blare from the DJ booth at the far end of the room. Questions are crowding my mind.

'You look a bit shocked; do you need to sit down?' Sasha has taken my arm and is steering me towards a chair before I've even had a chance to reply.

'I'm fine, I'm fine,' I say, waving away my eldest daughter's concern.

I find myself being lowered gently onto a velvet-covered chair. If I'm being honest, my legs do feel a little wobbly so I'm grateful for a chance to sit. I genuinely had no idea I would be thrust into the limelight for my birthday and the whole thing is overwhelming. I keep breathing in and out slowly, hoping the wave of emotions will settle down.

'She's not fine,' I hear Sasha saying over the top of my head. 'I'm not sure this was a good idea.'

'Stop fretting, she'll be up dancing soon enough.' Leah, my youngest daughter, is by my side now as well. I lean back in the chair and observe that Sasha and Leah are currently locked in a staring match. Sasha's lips are set in a disapproving line and Leah has her arms folded across her chest.

'It was a lovely surprise,' I say, smiling at them in the most reassuring way I can, trying to break the tension between them.

I know they both worry about me since Erin went missing and I understand why they're making a fuss of me this birthday. A few years ago, just weeks shy of the big seven-o milestone birthday, I was diagnosed with breast cancer. The months that followed were a fight for survival and the chemotherapy I had completely wiped my energy levels. I wasn't sure if my days were up and it's only really been in the last eight or nine months that finally I've felt fully recovered and more myself. I'm in remission and I'm guessing my girls wanted me to have the celebration I didn't get.

It was really sweet of them to do this, which is why I pull myself together and rise to my feet. I'm sure it will have taken a lot of effort to organise everything and I'm determined to put my misgivings about the date of this celebration to one side. I know I'm lucky to have reached seventy-five, so I resolve to make the most of the evening. I push away my doubts and instead smile brightly at my grown-up daughters. I'm sure they must be behind the surprise party.

'Are you sure you don't want to rest for a bit longer?' Sasha asks. She's always been the maternal, caring one of my three girls and the natural worrier as well.

'Let's go and have fun!' I fist-punch the air comically, with as much enthusiasm as I can muster.

Leah laughs. 'See, she's still got it!'

'I should go and say hello to everyone,' I start to say.

'Absolutely, but first of all Ophelia has a dress she wants you to wear,' Leah says.

'Of course she does.' I smile. I should've known that my fashion-obsessed granddaughter would have an outfit selected for me.

Leah ushers me towards the door but I'm stopped on my way out by some of the guests. My best friend Kim and her husband Matt sing a little chorus of 'Happy Birthday' to me and then my gym friends descend on me with open arms and warm hugs. Leah successfully disentangles me and we make our way to one of the plush bathrooms on the ground floor. She locks the main door to the bathroom so we have the mirrored area and several cubicles to ourselves. On the door to the cubicle at the far end, I see a dark blue full-length dress hanging up and a pair of matching shoes on the floor below it.

'There we are.' Leah gestures. 'This is for you.'

'That's a bit posh, isn't it?' I half-giggle. I don't think I've ever worn such a fancy dress in my life, not even for Sasha's remarriage.

'You deserve it,' Leah gushes.

'You don't think... well, you don't think I'm a bit past all this?' I raise my eyebrows.

'Nonsense, you're younger at heart than Sasha is.'

I don't respond to the jibe towards her sister but instead go and inspect the dress. It's my favourite colour and I'm secretly excited to slip into the material. I disappear into the cubicle with it and, miracle of miracles, it fits me perfectly.

'How's this?' I say, stepping out of the cubicle and giving a little twirl.

'Gorgeous!' Leah exclaims. 'You just need the shoes to complete the outfit.'

Leah helps me into the not-too-high shoes and then gets me to sit on a conveniently placed chair so she can do my make-up. She produces a cosmetics bag that's bursting at the seams, and it reminds me of her old life as a social media influencer. She used to get millions of lifestyle freebies and, as a result, she's well versed in different clothing and make-up brands. She pulls out a make-up brush and I sit patiently as she paints some colour onto my face.

'You look a million dollars,' Leah tells me as she points me towards the mirror.

My reflection certainly looks a cut above my usual hurried lick of mascara and dash of lipstick. 'Ah, thank you, love. You can come and do my make-up every morning if you like.'

We both laugh.

'Leah, thank you for organising all of this. It's good of you to—'

'I didn't organise this.'

'You didn't?'

'Nope, it wasn't me. Sorry, I wasn't sure if you'd want something like this... especially here.' Leah waves her hand around to indicate our surroundings and she doesn't need to elaborate any further.

'Oh, was it Sasha then?' I ask, the logical conclusion being that my other daughter was behind the planning of this event.

But Leah shakes her head, a ripple of uncertainty passing across her features.

If neither of my daughters organised this surprise party, then who did? Has another member of my friends or family gone to the trouble of setting all of this up? And if so, why today of all days?

I've got a bad feeling about this...

Chapter Four

Ophelia

While everyone is busy enjoying the party, I'm going to search for something in my mum's old study. It's usually locked and the only room in the hotel I don't have free access to. It's also the only room that hasn't been redecorated during the most recent refurb here. Since my dad was killed and my mum went missing, my grandfather Hugo has ordered several different repaints and upgrades to the hotel. I think it's because he can't stand coming here to the building where his son died, so he keeps changing things.

He's told me that he'll be relieved to hand the deeds over to me and Jasper once we've turned eighteen. Jasper has no interest in Burcott House but I can't wait to take it over and put my own stamp on the place. I also want to revive some of the projects my mum started, like the lavender products she worked hard to create. They were really popular with the guests and I'm sure I can make some money selling them at the hotel and online. It feels like the right time to do this.

I managed to get hold of a copy of the skeleton keys for the hotel earlier today, including the tiny silver key that unlocks my mum's study. I dip my hand into my pocket and feel the cool metal against my skin. Anticipation burns in my stomach as I glide down the corridor. I check over my shoulder, but there isn't anyone else in this section of the hotel. The guests are either at the bar getting drinks or milling around outside so I figure this is my chance.

I insert the key into the lock, hoping there might be at least one clue in this room to fill in the gaps in my family's history. I slip into the office and immediately open the blind. The window looks over the lavender fields; this room was my mum's favourite place in the whole hotel and I can see why. The rolling fields are stunning, and you can also see the path to our cute four-bed family cottage which lies just beyond the sea of purple flowers.

Coming into this room is like stepping back into a time capsule. I drift towards by the mantelpiece and look at the photographs of my family, images of my childhood and my parents' marriage. We all looked really happy. I skim my finger over one of the picture frames and a layer of dust comes away. The whole room needs a good clean; I doubt anyone has been in here for months. I don't like the idea of the hotel staff coming in and disturbing things, so I make a mental note to sort things out myself. As soon as I turn eighteen, no-one will be able to stop me. I guess I could've waited until next week to do this but I have a motive for wanting to come into this room sooner...

Sitting down at my mum's desk, I pull open the top drawer. There are tons of old files in here. Inside are colour-coded sections – from company accounts to future plans for the hotel. My mum was always very organised and it makes me feel fuzzy inside to see these files, each one like a small piece of her personality just resting in this room.

Opening the other wooden drawers, I'm hoping to find items more personal to her, maybe a diary or letters, but everything is related to the hotel business. I flip through the paperwork, just in case I'm missing anything, but there's nothing but numbers and checklists. I'm disappointed and it dawns on me I might not find anything that gives me new information about my parents.

I bang my fist down on the desk.

I've spent hours and hours scouring the internet to find out the truth about what happened to my parents when any one of my family members could've told me more. I've read back through the newspaper articles and listened to gruesome true crime podcasts that cover all sorts of conspiracy theories. In one of them, the podcaster was convinced that my dad had faked his death for the insurance money and my mum had 'disappeared' to join him in some far-flung tax haven. For weeks, I fantasised about this being a reality. I dreamed of an expensive black car one day arriving at my boarding school to take me to a private jet and then on to my waiting, smiling parents and a new life overseas.

The desk is the main piece of furniture in the room, along with a desk chair, a bookcase and a small Ottoman seat with inbuilt storage. I lift up the seat and find an assortment of different blankets inside. I rummage through them but there's nothing else in this space. Replacing the seat, I recall how I used to love sitting here as a little girl, watching my mum as she worked. Staring at the Ottoman it makes me wonder if there are any other hidden compartments in this room.

I try the bookcase first. But, after a few minutes, it becomes clear the shelves of books unfortunately aren't going to swing open to reveal a secret room. I run my hands along the rows of hardbacks and paperbacks. There's more dust. Reading the titles on the spines, I absorb them more fully than I have done before. There are lots of business books, plenty of autobiographies and a handful of motivational style texts. Gliding my fingers along the middle row, I notice there's a gap between the otherwise tightly pressed books.

Sliding my fingers into the space, I find a small, silver key. My face lights up. Perhaps this will lead me to some answers. It was tucked away which suggests my mum didn't want this key to be easily found. I just need to find out what the key opens. Looking around the room, I decide to move the mirror and two paintings off the walls, in case there's anything behind them. I do this carefully, not wanting to break anything. But there's nothing behind them except smoothly plastered walls so I replace the items just as gently.

The silver key must open something in here. I pull almost everything in the room out of its place, even shunting the heavy wooden desk along to see if there's anything under it. But I find nothing. I stamp my foot in annoyance. Why is nothing in my life straight-forward...

I bite my lip. I'm convinced there must be a clue in this room that will get me closer to understanding why my dad died and my mum went missing. Kicking the floor with my shoe, I stub my toe.

'Ouch,' I mutter. Looking down, I see the large, patterned rug. Dropping down to my knees, I push the rug aside and examine the floorboards beneath it. Running my hands over one of the floorboards, I discover it is loose.

'Yes!' I exclaim to myself.

Working quickly, I prise the board up and find the board next to it also comes free. Here I find a silver safe inset into the floor. My stomach flutters with excitement, perhaps I've finally found what I'm looking for.

Inserting the silver key from the bookcase into the safe lock, I discover that it fits perfectly. The safe door is a little stiff but, after some fumbling, I manage to get it open. Diving my hand inside, I pull out a photograph of my mum with Sasha, Leah and Jesse. They all look really young in the image, probably not much older than I am now. I place it on the floor next to me.

Then I find another silver key, it's smaller than the one that opened the safe. I turn it over in my hand, wondering what it might unlock. The next item I pull out of the safe is a small, leather-bound book with a tiny silver lock. It looks like it could be a diary. Excitedly, I insert the little key into the lock – it fits! I twist it and hear a satisfying noise as the lock clicks open.

But as I flip the book cover over my heart drops. The majority of the pages in this diary have been torn out, leaving just blank pages and the leather shell of the book. Why would someone do this? In my bones I feel as though the contents of this diary would've given me some answers.

Frustration surges through me, but I keep going. Rummaging around in the safe, I find a paper money clip with no money in but there's nothing else. It's clear someone has been in here before me and deliberately emptied this safe.

And I can guess who it was.

My grandmother Nadia. I'm certain she will have emptied this room of anything that shone any light on my mum's disappearance – I'm also certain she would've made sure it was clear of anything she didn't want the police to see at the time of the investigation. It's ironic that she has this ridiculous saying of there being 'no more secrets' in our family but she's just deluded. She must know the truth of what's gone on in the past, and my aunts Leah and Sasha probably do too, but they all remain very tight-lipped whenever I ask a question about my mum or the day that she went missing.

Sighing, I shut the safe and replace the rug. Then I tidy up, making sure that everything looks as it did when I came in here.

I have a complicated relationship with my grandmother and my aunts. There is no denying they've been there for me since both my parents died, especially my grandmother and Sasha. They call me at least once a week, and they've always dedicated their time to us during the school breaks. But can I trust them?

On the windowsill, I notice there is a photograph of my dad and my grandfather Hugo. They're wearing their skiing outfits. All of my family were keen skiers, and I can remember learning on the slopes in France from a young age with Jasper. None of us have been skiing since my mother went missing. I stare at the photograph, memories of the magical, snowy holidays coming back to me from the time before I was orphaned.

My paternal grandfather Hugo is technically my legal guardian now but he made it clear that he wasn't about to alter his life when he acquired two orphan grandchildren. He made the decision to send me and my twin brother to boarding school. I hate him for that almost as much as I hated boarding school.

Sasha has stepped into the role of my surrogate mother and over the years I desperately wanted to go and live with her. My grandfather wouldn't allow it though and I've been angry at him so many times because of this. Lately, I'm beginning to question if his decision to ship me off to school was just because he wanted me to have the best education or if there was more to it. I know he doesn't like Nadia or my aunts. I used to think it was because they're not really the sort of people he spends time with. He's used to rubbing shoulders with the upper classes, minor royals, and celebrities who have a lot of money. His world is very different to the Bailey family's.

I do know that my mum didn't speak to her family for years. No-one would tell me why – not even her. Just like Leah won't tell me why she has a scar on her face, and Sasha refuses to discuss the murder her ex-husband Jesse committed. Again, I think that my grandmother must know the truth about everything. I'd thought that as I got older, they would share the past with me but the longer they've remained silent, the more I've wondered whether there are things they don't want me to find out about.

If they can keep secrets, so can I.

I grin to myself because I have a very big secret that I've been keeping for months. This party is the perfect place to reveal it.

And I can't wait to tell everyone...

Chapter Five

Nadia

Feeling faint for the second time today, I bite down on my tongue so hard I can taste the metallic tang of blood in my mouth. But it does the trick and shocks me enough to chase away the woozy fog that was descending over me.

'Do you know for certain that Sasha didn't organise this party?'

Leah chews her lip. 'Umm, I'm not sure actually.' She looks thoughtful, twisting a strand of her corn-coloured hair around her finger. 'I haven't caught up with Sasha properly; work has been very busy and I was a little late arriving.' She looks a bit sheepish at this admission. 'I just about got through the door before you pulled up in your car,' she says with honesty.

I smile; promptness has never been my youngest daughter's strength.

'It must have been Sasha,' I say, trying to convince myself. Although the fact Leah didn't have anything to do with putting together the surprise party or any knowledge of her sister's involvement makes me doubt this. Sasha and Leah may not see each other on a weekly basis but they're always on the phone or messaging one another.

'I'm sure Ophelia must have gone on at Sasha about having a party and she probably thought combining the two birthdays was a good idea.'

Leah makes a non-committal noise in response.

'You don't think so?'

Fiddling with a button on her dress, Leah says, 'Maybe, I just don't know if Sasha would use this place as a venue...'

Silence fills the space between us. Sasha finds it just as difficult coming to Burcott House. It's hard for her not to think about her ex-husband Jesse – what she found out about him and what he did at the Christmas party here almost ten years ago.

'Excuse me, nature calls,' I say to Leah as I make a beeline for one of the toilet cubicles. I slide the lock and then lean heavily against the door. My thoughts are already leaping five steps ahead on who else could possibly have pulled off setting all of this up. I pinch the bridge of my nose with my forefingers and try to think clearly.

Sasha has been like a surrogate mother to Ophelia since Erin disappeared so there is a chance that Ophelia has persuaded her to throw a party here. Ophelia has a knack of twisting us all around her little finger.

Aaron's father, Hugo Scott has certainly provided well for Ophelia and Jasper financially as their legal guardian: they haven't wanted for anything and have been thoroughly spoiled by their doting grandfather. But whenever Ophelia and Jasper were home from school breaks, Hugo lacked the experience to deal with temper tantrums and friendship dramas and preferred to spend the majority of his day on the golf course attached to Burcott House. Sasha and I both stepped into the void as mentors, role models and shoulders to cry on for the two teenagers as they grew up. Sasha took a firm hand on discipline – after all she's a headmistress in her day job – but Ophelia has won a soft spot in her heart and it's likely she may have been persuaded by her niece to throw the party here.

'Well,' I say, breaking the silence as I emerge from the cubicle. 'I'll ask Sasha later.' I reach for the hand moisturiser. 'Let's go, shall we?'

Leah grins back at me. 'Of course.'

We enter through the double doors into the Winchester Room and I can see the activity has kicked up a notch. Most people have a glass in hand and music is playing in the backdrop.

'I forgot to give you this,' Leah says, handing me a blue eye mask. 'Ophelia told me the theme is a masquerade ball and there's going to be dancing and entertainment later.'

I take the mask and slip it into the small blue handbag Leah also furnished me with. 'I'll put it on later,' I reply, telling myself that Ophelia must've had a hand in organising the celebrations after all, because she and I both enjoy period dramas. We love settling on the sofa together and immersing ourselves in anything involving swoony romances and big dresses, so this has my granddaughter's taste written all over it.

This idea feels reassuring and brings a smile to my face. I'm sure there must be a perfectly straightforward explanation behind who organised this birthday party, and I'm bound to find out soon enough, but I'm going to be on edge until I know. I swish towards a waitress holding a drinks tray, all the while peering around the room to for my eldest daughter.

I'm determined to uncover who's behind tonight's celebration, so I can put my mind at ease. Then I'm going to have a few drinks and try to work out how I deal with the real reason I turned up at Burcott House today.

Because I've got some unfinished business to attend to...

Chapter Six

Sasha

'Stop!' I half-shout as I shoot my hand out to try and prevent the accident that's about to happen. In my job as a headmistress, I'm used to having eyes in the back of my head and anticipating potential disasters where teenagers are concerned. But even so, none of my teacher training has prepared me for the whirlwind that is my six-year-old son, Fergus. His mop of curly, red-brown hair hurtles past me and I just about prevent him crashing into the nearby chocolate fountain.

'Woah!' I exclaim. 'That was a near miss! What were you doing?'

I pull him a decent distance away from the flowing chocolate but when I look at his face properly, I can see his bottom lip is beginning to wobble.

'What's the matter?'

'Mummy, I was scared!' Tears start to spill down his flushed cheeks and I pull him into my embrace.

'Scared? Why, my sweetheart?'

I shudder, not wanting to admit that Burcott House still gives me the chills and I've had a creeping sense of dread growing since we arrived. The only time I come here is to see my niece Ophelia and nephew Jasper when they're home from boarding school. Even then,

I try to engineer it so that I'm picking them up to take them out somewhere or bringing them back to my home.

'Fergus?' I press him. The longer I have to wait for an answer, the more my mind goes into overdrive about what might have spooked him. 'Can you tell me what's happened?'

His head is buried in the folds of my dress and his response is just a mumble. I step back and drop down to my knees. 'What was that?'

'The masks.' Fergus whimpers, pointing his finger over my shoulder.

I turn to look and see there's a group of men wearing garish masks over their faces. They're pretty ghoulish and not at all the type of thing suitable for a masquerade ball.

'Oh, it's OK,' I say, looking into his worried little face. 'It's just grown-ups being silly. Look,' I try to divert his attention. 'Mummy has this pretty mask with gemstones on it.' I produce my own from a conveniently and practically designed deep pocket in my black dress. 'And here's yours,' I tell him as I place the child's penguin mask into his hand. I couldn't get anything else in his size and I thought the black and white penguin design would look cute with his smart mini tux.

'Can I put it on?' he asks brightly.

'Sure you can!' I wipe away his tears and help him get the mask on. 'Can you do a penguin walk for me?'

He nods enthusiastically and starts off at a waddle.

'Very good, but away from the chocolate fountain!' I warn him, steering him towards the tall, handsome man coming towards us.

'Sasha!' My new husband Douglas picks me an inch off the floor and spins me round.

'Hey,' I say softly.

'I made it, sorry I couldn't be here at the start – was Nadia surprised?'

I give him a quick kiss on the lips before answering, and he kisses me back in earnest. I still can't quite believe how much my life has changed since we got together. Every day I'm grateful I met Douglas. I was at rock bottom after the Christmas Party here all those years ago – the one that we don't talk about, but I think about all the time. The night when I discovered my ex-husband Jesse was a cold-blooded murderer and that he was also having an affair with my sister Erin. That was why he pushed her husband Aaron off the spiral staircase to his death. A crime of passion, or so he pleaded in the court case.

The aftermath of that party wasn't easy. Jesse's arrest drove me to a dark place. Then Erin disappeared just over a month later on our ill-fated family skiing trip. I was one of the last people to see her, and there are some things that happened that day of the snowstorm that are hard to forget. But I wasn't the only one who suffered. Poor Ophelia and Jasper had one parent dead and the other presumed dead within the space of a few months.

Fergus waddles madly and Douglas laughs loudly. I can't help but join in. The scene in front of me contrasting with my thoughts of the past.

The challenges our family went through were considerable and trying to start again was a struggle. I wasn't able to work for a while; my head was all over the place and there was no way I could function properly in a demanding professional role at school. I'd also been drinking heavily to blot out the trauma, which only made things even worse.

'And has the penguin been behaving himself?' Douglas enquires, I nod in response.

I thank my lucky stars for another chance in life. I met Douglas at an AA meeting. Or to be accurate, just outside the rundown community centre where the meeting was taking place. I was hovering on the threshold and about to turn around and go home when Douglas saw me wavering and helped me through the door. At first, I assumed he was another alcoholic looking to sort out his addiction. But it soon became clear that he was the class leader, and not one of the participants.

'Are we diving into this chocolate fountain or what?' Douglas asks, his broad Scottish accent sending a delicious tremor down my spine.

'You first,' I encourage. Douglas doesn't wait to be told twice and is soon spearing strawberries onto the end of a stick and shoving them into the dripping chocolatey goodness.

Honestly, I think Douglas was the only reason I kept going back to those meetings. It worked and, with his help, I managed to kick my regular evening drinking sessions and get my life back on track quickly. I swore I would never trust another man again after what Jesse did but meeting Douglas changed all of that. I take him in, his bushy brown beard and kind hazel eyes. Douglas is the type of person you trust the moment he starts speaking in his deep Scottish accent, and it's because of him I've been able to see the good in others once again.

Fergus tugs on my dress and I know he's about to ask me if he can have some too.

'Go ahead sweetie,' I encourage him. His face beams with delight.

Fergus is a ray of sunshine in our lives. I watch Douglas bend to pick our boy up so that he can reach to spear strawberries on a little wooden stick before dunking them in the waterfall of chocolate. Douglas is an amazing father to our son; he loves being a daddy. And he's also a brilliant father figure to my daughter Freya as well as to my niece Ophelia and my nephew Jasper. I couldn't imagine life without him and, finally, I'm the happiest version of myself.

I'm distracted as I catch sight of my mother gliding across the room towards me. She's glowing with health and my heart leaps to see her looking so well. The blue colouring of her dress is a shade she often wears and the dress suits her perfectly.

'Have fun darling,' I say to Fergus and leave him in Douglas's arms with a bowl in his hand and a smile on his face.

'You look incredible!' I tell my mother.

'Thank you – and so do you,' she responds.

My black dress is simple and nothing too fancy, but it's elegant and, as I approach my fifth decade on this earth, I finally feel comfortable in my own skin so I take the compliment instead of batting it away.

'Sasha, this must have taken you hours to prepare and you kept it all so quiet! I had no idea whatsoever, thank you,' my mother is saying. Her words come out in a hurry.

'Mum,' I cut in before she can go any further. 'I didn't plan this.'

Mum stops and looks at me like she's trying to work out whether I'm trying to pull the wool over her eyes.

'I would never have set up a party at Burcott House.' My eyes fix on the internal doors that lead to the sweeping marble staircase to emphasise my meaning.

'It really wasn't you?' Nadia quizzes me. 'I assumed it must've been you or Leah, but your sister says it wasn't her either. And if it wasn't either of you, then who was it?'

I had been wondering the exact same thing and the conclusion I'd come to was that my niece Ophelia probably twisted her rich grandfather around her little finger and persuaded him to throw a party here. I'm sure he would've been reluctant – after all, the last family party held here resulted in his son's untimely death – but maybe she got him onside by insisting that the celebrations weren't just for her but for Nadia too. That must be the explanation.

Turning my head, I try to catch a glimpse of Ophelia's distinctive pink dress but I can't see it. I share my assumption with my mother and she turns the idea over thoughtfully.

'Yes, you're right, that's it, Sasha. It's just the sort of thing that Ophelia would do.'

My mother is flustered and I'm not certain that she's reassured. 'Mum, what's going on?'

'Nothing,' she says, too quickly.

'No more secrets, remember?'

As a family, we'd made a pact after Erin went missing. My mother, Leah and I swore to each other that there would be no more family secrets – there had been too many, and the only way we were going to move forward was if we were truthful with each other.

She gives me a weak smile in response. 'I know, I know.'

Tucking my hand into her arm, she declares, 'Let's search for Ophelia and we can find out exactly what she's been getting up to.'

I nod in agreement and follow her. But why is my stomach sinking? And why do I feel like my mother's hiding something?

Chapter Seven

Ophelia

Heading back into the Winchester Room, I wave at a few friends as I dodge past groups of guests taking advantage of the free glasses of alcohol. I don't stop to talk; I make my way straight through to the gardens. It's still light and warm out: the perfect night for a summer party.

I stop to snap a photo on my phone, it's going to look incredible on my socials. There's always a stunning view from the hotel: the rose garden is so gorgeous in full bloom and the rolling hills of lavender around the building are dreamy.

The terrace has never looked so good. There are pretty, twinkling fairy lights twisted around the wooden pergola and in the trees nearby. The amount of seating has doubled from what's usually on offer for our hotel guests and there's plenty of choice, from tall wooden stools and a high-top wooden table in the covered pergola area to low, comfortable rattan sofas positioned to make the best of the view across the countryside. Along with the new seating, there's a number of different artisan food trucks, providing everything from pizza to ice cream and crêpes.

If Jasper was here, he'd be absolutely loving this. He's such a foodie and he'd be trying everything he could.

I head to the pizza truck and ask for a small margherita. The smell wafting through the air is delicious, making my tummy rumble.

I pull out my purse and ask, 'How much?'

'No need; it's all been paid for.' The woman behind the counter, her hair scraped back into a messy ponytail, winks at me. 'And we were paid very nicely for this gig!'

I raise my eyebrow; a huge amount of expense must've gone into this evening. As I wait for my pizza, my thoughts turn to Jasper again. I phoned him a few months ago and asked him if he'd be coming back to England for our big birthday, but he just made excuses about his studies. I've put the pressure on since then too because I wanted him to be here. I've guilt tripped him on our recent calls as well as trying everything else I could think of to get him to come home. But, for the first time ever, he has been really stubborn. He dug his heels in and refused to come back. I know he's enjoying life in America, and he's already told me he doesn't want to live in England any time soon. He finds it hard being here, especially at Burcott House.

I sigh. He's hurt me, without realising it. I always imagined he'd be around if I needed him – and we've needed each other a lot in recent years. But Jasper has found distance the best escape from our family's past. He's charged forward without me on his own path, away from our childhood home – and our grief. Recently, I've come to accept that I'm just going to have to get used to being a solo twin and figure out my own future.

'Here you go,' the woman with the ponytail hands me a warm cardboard box. 'Enjoy!'

'I will do, thanks!' I smile back at her.

There's lots of people out here but I'm pretty hungry so I sit down in one of the garden chairs on the lawn, in a quiet spot under the shade of an old oak tree. Eagerly, I flip the cardboard lid open and tear off a slice of the pizza. Then I shovel the yummy cheese and tomato pizza into my mouth.

'Ouch.' I chew quickly and swallow the too-hot mouthful. The gooey, molten cheese has burnt my tongue. It's my own fault for being too impatient but the shock still makes my eyes water.

I hurry over to one of the other trucks and get a plastic cup of lemonade, gulping it down fast to try and cool my mouth. I of course knew what was going to happen when I started eating the hot food but I did it anyway. How is it that I manage to get myself into tricky situations even though I can often see them coming?

Settling back down into my chair, I wait a few minutes and I'm then able to eat the pizza and enjoy it this time without hurting myself. This feels like a moment of calm in what is otherwise going to be a full-on evening. Tucking a strand of hair behind my ear, I allow myself to admire my surroundings.

Seeing the potential of Burcott House tonight does give me a little fizz of excitement. My mum used to run a wedding business here as well as the hotel side of things. That all fell by the wayside without her, but I have dreams of hosting weddings here again. The idea of two people in love spending their special day here and filling the place with happiness, laughter and love is exactly what I want.

For too long this building became associated with my dad's murder. Burcott House was shut for months and months. My grandfather Hugo refused to reopen it until he realised just how expensive the running costs of a place like this were and then reluctantly agreed to open the hotel once more. For the first year or two we had lots of bookings from the kind of people who like to spend the night in a haunted house and we were even contacted by a company that proposed to run a ghost tour here. I can remember Grandfather shouting down the phone at that request. After a while, the interest faded and, as usual, people's attention was captured by the next news story. Our regular customers gradually filtered back, word of mouth spread on how gorgeous the place is and the hotel is now just as busy as it used to be.

I fiddle with the silver necklace I'm wearing, which belonged to my mum. There are two little stars nestled next to a big star in between them. In the last conversation I had with her, she told me she liked to imagine they represented the three of us – she was the big star and Jasper and I were the two little stars either side. I smile at the sweet memory. I wanted to wear the necklace tonight so that she felt close to me at this significant celebration.

'Ophelia! Isn't this the best!' my cousin Freya squeals at me. She flings her arms around me and gives me such a tight hug that it leaves me breathless.

Freya is my cousin but, more than that, she's like the sister I never had. People often mistake her for my twin as we look so similar and if Jasper is with us, everyone assumes we must be triplets.

'Hey,' I nod to the tall guy behind Freya. His name is Levi and he's been Freya's boyfriend for the last few months; she's absolutely besotted with him and it's not hard to see why. His sandy-coloured fringe falls over his handsome face and he gives off a relaxed, casual vibe in his plain white shirt and jeans. He nods back at me.

'How on earth did you manage to get this past your grandfather?' Freya gushes.

I shrug. 'What do you mean?'

'Come off it,' Freya laughs. 'This whole party, you've organised it – right?'

'No,' I reply, a little too forcefully.

'Really?' Freya pouts and then starts checking off reasons on her fingers. 'You've wanted an eighteenth birthday party since forever, you're constantly going on about turning this place into an events business, and the theme is a masquerade ball. How does this not have your name stamped all over it?'

'You've got it wrong,' I try to say.

'Oh, I get it. You didn't ask permission from your grandfather and you don't want to get into trouble.' She winks at me. 'That's why it was a surprise, wasn't it? Genius!'

'Wait, that's not it.'

But Freya isn't listening; she's convinced she's right.

'Well,' she says. 'I'm impressed.' She hooks an arm through mine, still chattering away. 'And you've got my attention. You know you were talking about me working with you here, on weddings and stuff? I've been thinking about it and I agree it could be kinda cool to do. I'm in.'

'What? Seriously?' I'm surprised. Sasha – Freya's mother and my aunt – has been against this idea. Sasha wants Freya to go to university and get more qualifications. Freya doesn't usually go against what her mum wants so I didn't think she'd go for my idea.

So far, Sasha has been nothing but negative when I mention hosting events here. She's been quick to talk about how much work would be needed. That's because my aunt is convinced she can persuade me to go to university but I've already decided that's not for me. I've spent half my life at boarding school so I just want the chance to put roots down in my own home.

'Yeah, I was thinking I'd take a year out before throwing loads of money at uni. And we'd be a great team,' Freya says.

'We would,' I beam. 'That's what I keep telling you!' This has made me so happy. I can start to see a plan for my future forming. 'Let's get some drinks in a bit to celebrate!'

'Yay!' Freya squeezes me again before grabbing Levi's hand and tugging him towards a group of their friends.

A warm glow spreads through me at the idea of Freya and I working together. With Jasper in America, Freya has become even more important to me.

We mostly get on well. Like anyone with a sibling-style relationship, we fall out now and again. I have to admit, I'm often the one who causes the arguments. Usually, it's over something small and mostly because Freya can't see how lucky she is. I would've given anything for a normal upbringing. Living under the same roof as the rest of my family, with my mother still alive, is the thing I've wished for the most. Freya constantly moans about Sasha and it makes me so mad. She obsesses over silly arguments and Sasha's strict rules and she's oblivious to how much her mother loves her.

Some days I've wanted to switch places with Freya; like those two girls in that old movie, *The Parent Trap*. I'd give up all of the money in my bank accounts for a different life. But maybe turning eighteen and leaving school will be a new phase for me and one that I get to be in control of.

Wandering past the food trucks, I come to an area to the side of the house that's been set up with entertainment. There's a fire-eater warming up, practising taking great gulps of fire on a mini stage. A group of my grandmother's friends are cheering, clearly easily pleased. There's a face-painter transforming my cousin Fergus's sweet little face into a glittery version of something from the animal kingdom, while a magician is putting on a top hat and reorganising a battered suitcase to the side of the stage. There's also another group of entertainers in shiny leotards who have just arrived.

But the thing that gets my attention is the small, scruffy wagon on wheels at the very end of this area. The faded words Tarot Reader can just about be made out on the side of the wagon. I shiver a little in the sunshine. I have a strange feeling this is where I need to be so I climb the steps and knock on the half-open door.

After all, what I want more than anything is to find out the truth. I want to know what really happened to my parents. Lately, I've been piecing things together and there are many things that don't add up. So many lies that I've been told by people I trusted.

Who knows if this Tarot reader is the real deal or not, but maybe talking to someone who doesn't know my family would be helpful.

I'll try anything that will help me to crack open the secrets of my family's past...

Chapter Eight

Nadia

My niece, Hayley Bailey, comes over and kisses me on the cheek. Her husband and three young daughters are trailing just behind her. Hayley asks me how I am and congratulates me on my birthday.

'Thank you,' I say. And then we're off, questions and answers flying between us. It's always so easy to chat to Hayley. Part way through our conversation, my attention is drawn towards rosy-cheeked Jenny, Hayley's youngest. The small child is peeking out from behind her mother's legs. Whenever I see this particular family, it reminds me of being a mother of three little girls. I get flashbacks of the chaos and the sleep deprivation and the laughter that come with having young children. It's true what they say, the days are long but the years are short. It was forever ago now and yet I still hold the memories close in my heart.

'How are you?' I exclaim, as Andrew, Hayley's long-term partner and father of the three girls, leans in to give me a polite kiss on the cheek.

'Very well, thank you. Happy birthday to you!' Andrew replies cheerfully.

I can't help but compare this family to my own situation. Hayley has the support of a loving – and good, honest – man to help her raise their children. My experience was very different: for the most part I single-handedly raised my brood. Something I'm very proud of, and the importance of being a strong, independent woman is a lesson I tried to instil in the three young daughters I was bringing up. Although I can't deny life was difficult. I struggled to make ends meet and there were some days when I wasn't sure if I could keep on going. But we made it through. Leah is now a sought-after journalist, living in a stunning apartment in London, Sasha is a headteacher with a family of her own, and I managed to pay off the mortgage on my little terrace house – my safe haven is finally mine. But I regret that things went so wrong with Erin...

I'm making small talk with my niece when something occurs to me.

'Hayley, who invited you to the party?'

Hayley and her family live in Cornwall, right at the very bottom near Land's End. We don't see each other often because we live over three hours away from each other but we keep in touch fairly regularly. She's my brother's child. For several decades, my brother Samson and I lost touch; he'd disapproved of my relationship with my ex-partner Craig. I couldn't bear to admit he had been right when Craig was carted off to prison for killing a man during a robbery that went wrong. But Samson has been in a nursing home with dementia for the last five years and I've made sure to be there for my niece. We've actually grown closer than I ever expected to be possible after the decades of estrangement between my brother and I. Whoever organised this party would have to know that because Hayley isn't someone who I see in person, or even interact with on social media; our contact is via old-fashioned letters and phone calls.

Hayley frowns at me quizzically. 'We got an invite through the post.'

'Did it say who it was from?'

She licks her lips. 'I don't think so... hang on.' She delves into her brightly coloured handbag, a patchwork of every shade of every colour you could imagine. 'I've got it here.'

She hands the invite over to me, which is printed on expensive thick paper. One side is cream-coloured and the wording on it gives the details of a celebration party for my seventy-fifth birthday and Ophelia's eighteenth, along with the address of Burcott House and a note in bold to make it very clear that neither of us are to be told about the party before it happens. There are no details about the sender included.

I'm shocked because if the party was a surprise for Ophelia too then it means she couldn't have been behind organising it. At first, I thought it unlikely my granddaughter would intentionally arrange to share her birthday moment with an oldie like me, as she loves to be the centre of attention. Her twin brother, Jasper, is the total opposite. He's shy and unassuming, and currently studying in America – which is probably a good thing as he would've hated a big-scale celebration like this. Although Ophelia and I have had a special bond since her mother went missing so I had wondered if maybe she'd included me in her birthday plans because of our relationship. But the invite suggests I'm wrong and she had nothing to do with today's celebrations.

Turning the piece of card over in my hand, I almost drop it in disbelief. The other side is a shimmering, golden colour. I blink in disbelief. Not many people will remember this but when Erin sent out the invites to her fateful Christmas party, the envelopes were a similar colour. I know because I kept both the envelope and the invite. At the time, they were a beacon of hope, a long-awaited message from my estranged daughter who hadn't spoken to me in years. Am I reading too much into this? Is it just a coincidence these are the same unusual colour? Or is this someone's idea of a sick joke?

'Is something wrong?' Hayley asks me.

'No... no, I don't think so,' I say, not wishing to alarm my niece. 'Would you mind if I kept this?'

'Of course not,' Hayley replies, sounding a little confused.

'As a memento of the evening.'

Hayley brightens at this. 'A lovely idea.' She then turns to her three girls – Jenny, Charlotte and Rachel – and bends down to speak to them. 'What do you say to your Auntie Nadia?'

'Happy birthday!' the three of them chime together. Jenny then goes back to hiding behind her mother's legs while Charlotte and Rachel suddenly have their attention captured by the sight of the chocolate fountain just behind me.

'It's delicious,' I tell them conspiratorially. 'Go and help yourselves.'

They don't need to be told twice, and the mischievous pair scamper off together.

Hayley and I agree to meet on the dance floor a little bit later. Clutching the shiny invite in my hand, I continue my search for Ophelia. I haven't seen her indoors at all so I decide to head into the garden to see if she's there.

The sky's still blue, although it's deepening now, and as soon as I go outside, I'm hit by the sweet, sickly scent of burnt sugar. There's already a small, snaking queue forming next to the food truck selling

I knew it. I knew something was going to go horribly wrong today. I haven't been able to shake this feeling since I stepped through the door of Burcott House earlier.

The question is, who is screaming... and why?

Chapter Nine

Sasha

'What was that?'

Music is pumping through the main room at Burcott House but I swear I just heard someone scream. And I'm not the only one, other people around me are startled too. I clutch Douglas's arm.

'Did you just hear that? The scream?'

Douglas squints down at me, his eyes filled with concern. 'I didn't hear a thing.'

I don't wait to hear the rest of his sentence because I'm certain of what I heard. I peel away from him, dashing towards the garden. As soon as I'm outdoors I continue to accelerate towards the direction of the noise. I see my mother and she's springing into action, moving with several other people towards the large gate at the side of the garden which leads to the car park for the hotel.

'What was it? What happened?' I can't hide my panic as I grab my mother's arm and demand answers. She can see the alarm in my face but it's clear she knows no more than I do. A small crowd of people has gathered, whispering between themselves with concerned looks on their faces.

'It came from that direction.' She points as the front gate that leads into the car park area begins to swing open. They're electrically operated and from, where I'm standing, there's no way to tell who is coming in or going out of the high gates.

'Where are the girls?' I ask urgently. I still refer to my daughter Freya and my niece Ophelia as 'the girls' despite them being young women now, because they will forever remain my little girls.

'I've just been speaking with Freya, she's fine. I haven't seen Ophelia in a while,' my mother replies hurriedly.

My hands are shaking, it's ridiculous that I'm this jittery. Being back here makes me anxious and I can't get rid of the sense that something awful is about to happen. Hearing that scream flung me back into memories of that cold, winter night when my whole life splintered into a million pieces. As the large gates slowly pull apart, I want to run in the opposite direction. I don't want to see what caused that heart-stopping sound. Because I'm terrified that it could have the power to shatter the lives of the Bailey women once again.

And now, I have more to lose. Life has never been this good before – I'm blissfully, sickeningly happy and I know it. My marriage to Jesse was on the rocks even before I found out about his infatuation with Erin and the part he played in Aaron's death. But now... now I'm completely besotted with Douglas. He's shown me what true love really is.

I realise just how unhappy I was with Jesse and, even though I would never want to relive what our family went through, Douglas has been my silver lining. If Jesse hadn't done what he did, if we hadn't divorced, if I hadn't struggled and started drinking, then I would never have gone to the AA meeting where I met Douglas. I could still be stuck in an unhappy marriage. Instead, I'm here and, despite being pushed to my limit, I'm a survivor. I'm living the best version of my life. The idea that all of this is just too good to be true is one that keeps me lying awake at night. I have heart palpitations when I think that all of this could be taken away from me. And my fear is that my family will drag me back into a nightmare again...

The gates open and the small crowd collectively inhales sharply. I do the same, even though I can't quite see what's going on. There's a ripple of concern and then someone in front of me shifts and I see it. A sleek, ice-blue Mercedes is at right-angles in the car park – it's clear it must have swerved suddenly and sharply. My stomach clenches as I balance on my toes, craning my neck and trying to work out what's going on. All I can think is: please don't let it be Ophelia who is hurt.

There's a cluster of a few people just in front of the car, and it's obvious something has happened. But how bad is it? I move forward, praying that my niece hasn't been involved in this accident. I know Freya is OK because my mother has just spoken to her, but if anything happened to Ophelia I would be just as devastated. She's my surrogate daughter; I've taken her under my wing and cared for her like my own. I regard her as my responsibility and I worry about her just as much as my two biological children.

I jostle through, trying to get closer, and as I do one of the men leaning against the car turns around.

'It's OK, folks!' The man, wearing an exceptionally sharp suit, turns towards the crowd and speaks in a clear and reassuring tone. 'There's been a little bump but nothing serious.'

A murmur ripples around the party guests. Most of them are satisfied with this explanation and start to drift away, back to the food trucks and the entertainment. But not me. I've got to see who it is for myself.

'I'll go and check everyone's OK,' I say to my mother, who nods her approval.

Striding purposefully forward, I reach the handful of people gathered by the car. 'Do you need any help?' I offer. 'I'm first-aid trained.'

The man in the suit turns to me. 'An ambulance is on its way, just as a precaution.'

'Oh, do you need anything in the meantime?'

The man steps towards me and I get a glimpse of a young woman sitting on the bonnet of the Mercedes. But there's no flash of red hair – it's not Ophelia. Although she looks around the same age so it could be one of her friends.

The man shakes his head, a steely smile fixed to his face.

'Whose car is it?' I say, suddenly suspicious.

The smile becomes more fixed but the man doesn't falter. 'It's mine. The girl just stepped out in front of us, she's lucky my wife has quick reflexes.'

Something about this doesn't ring true to me. The man is oozing wealth and he's obviously used to taking control of situations. But who's the girl? And did she really step out in front of his flashy car?

'I think that's one of my niece's friends,' I garble, barging past him and charging towards the injured girl. 'Are you OK? Are you Ophelia's friend?' I ask, positioning myself close to the girl.

She nods back at me, tears spilling from her aquamarine-coloured eyes. 'I... I don't know what happened.'

Her hands are scuffed and her tights torn from where she's fallen. There's a cut on her forehead and I notice she's rubbing her right hip in a way that suggests it's painful.

'You're going to be all right,' I say reassuringly to her.

I look around at the man in the smart suit, who's chatting with a similarly dressed man and a woman wearing a white floor-length dress with silver straps. Her matching handbag is branded Dior and I'd place bets it's the real deal rather than a fake from a market stall. Neither of the men are ruffled by the accident but the woman is pacing agitatedly.

'My name is Sasha,' I say to the girl. 'I'm Ophelia's aunt. Do you know any of these people?' I nod towards the trio standing nearby.

'No. No... I don't,' she stutters in reply.

'What's your name?'

'Anne-Marie.' She's shivering, it must be from the shock as the weather is still pleasantly mild.

'Hey, could we get a loan of a jacket?' I direct my question towards the two men.

The guy who had spoken earlier shrugs off his suit jacket and places it around Anne-Marie's shoulders before going back to chat with his friend.

'You can tell me what happened,' I say to Anne-Marie in a low voice. I'm convinced there's more to it than the girl walking in front of the car without looking.

Anne-Marie glances worriedly at the three well-dressed people.

'It doesn't need to go any further,' I reassure her.

Anne-Marie in a whisper tells me, 'He was driving the car.' She nods towards the confident man who's just handed over his suit jacket. 'But they said I can't tell anyone that. I have to say it was the woman driving.'

'What? Why?' I ask.

She shrugs.

'That's wrong. If he was—'

'You said you wouldn't say anything,' Anne-Marie hisses back at me.

'That's right, I won't if you don't want me to but you don't have to lie for him. And if you change your mind, I'll support you.'

Anne-Marie sighs. 'No-one else saw. My word against his. Besides, he said he'll give me some money if I stick to his story.'

Internally I groan. This is all so wrong. This is how young people learn to lie, from older people who should know better. And this is just another situation where money wins, and not the truth.

'You don't have to go along with that, you can say what really happened,' I tell her gently.

Anne-Marie looks like she's about to weep. 'I've already agreed. He's given me his card.'

I want to shout at these people who think they can solve everything by paying others off. I want to show this young woman that this behaviour is not OK, and I want to make things right. But I can't betray Anne-Marie's trust.

'Did they say how long the ambulance would be?' I ask her, trying to keep calm.

Just as I finish my sentence, the peal of a siren cuts through the air. Thank goodness we didn't have long to wait. As the sound of the emergency services grows louder, my heart beats a little faster. This feels too much like déjà vu. Anne-Marie looks dazed, so I take her hand in mine. I try to keep focused on what's happening in the present, rather than letting my thoughts be drawn back to the past.

The ambulance speeds into the car park, just as Ophelia comes running towards her friend.

'Anne-Marie! Anne-Marie, are you hurt?'

Just behind Ophelia strides her grandfather Hugo Scott and his wife Melanie.

'What the hell is going on here?' Hugo demands, looking stony-faced. No doubt his thoughts are also leaping to the fatal incident that happened at the last party held at Burcott House.

Ophelia hugs her friend and I watch as the tiniest drop of blood falls from the small cut on Anne-Marie's head and splashes onto the pristine paintwork of the car.

'A small accident,' the suited man says to Hugo Scott, all confidence once more. 'The ambulance was called just as a precaution,' he repeats the same line he said to me. The two men clap each other on the back, and I note from their body language that they must be well-acquainted.

Anne-Marie mouths a 'thank you' to me as she's helped into the back of the emergency vehicle. I watch as she goes, hating that this young woman has been bullied into a lie and wishing I could do something about it. I know the damage lies can do, and I don't want to be party to it anymore. Perhaps she'll tell the truth once she's had longer to think about it.

The initial fear I had when hearing that scream has fizzled out but as I return to the gardens, where the party activities are ramping up a notch, the notion that it's not safe here enters my mind. I have a primal instinct that I should just go – before anything worse happens. I don't want to stay any longer than I need to. So I start to plan my exit. I'll need to stay at least until the cake is cut but, after that, I'm going to get out of here as soon as I possibly can. It'll be easy enough to get Douglas and Fergus to come with me, but I know Freya is going to be harder to prise away from the party. I don't want to spoil her evening but I need to go with the warning feeling deep in my heart and get my family away from this place.

Nothing good ever happens here, and I don't want to wait around to see what else is in store tonight.

Chapter Ten

Ophelia

'Ophelia, stop right there.'

I halt and spin round on my heels. 'Yes Grandfather?'

'Don't you "Yes Grandfather" me,' his deep voice booms back. 'You've got some explaining to do.'

'I have?' I say, looking as innocently as I can up at him.

'Yes, young lady, what is all this about?' He flings his arms wide. 'I told you that under no circumstances would there be a party held at Burcott House.'

'I know you did, which is why I'm surprised! Thank you for sorting this!' I smile sweetly.

His bushy grey eyebrows knit together. 'Thank you? Don't try to throw me off the scent and act like you had nothing to do with this.'

'But I didn't,' I insist, looping my arm through his as we walk back through the gates and into the garden.

'You didn't organise the ballgowns, the chocolate fountain or the fire-eater?'

I can feel his questioning stare on me. I answer assertively, just like he's taught me to do. 'No, I knew nothing about it. I thought that maybe you'd decided to make all my birthday wishes come true after all?' I cross my fingers behind my back and hope for the best.

My grandfather stops then and cups my face in his gnarled, old hands. 'Ophelia Bailey-Scott, did you or did you not contrive this party into being?'

'Well, I may have manifested *a lot* for a celebration like this to happen. I wrote in my morning journal every day for a month... But I didn't have anything to do with the bookings or anything like that.'

He draws back, hands on hips, and I notice his wife Melanie is approaching from the direction of the house. She's a bit younger than my grandfather and we get on well, she's usually on my side when my grandfather is being old-fashioned or stubborn. I wonder if it's crossed his mind that Melanie could be responsible for today. She could've organised it all, knowing me well enough to choose the things I'd like.

However, judging by her expression, it's obvious Melanie has nothing to do with this either. Her mouth is pinched and her arms are folded, she's not happy at all. I don't think I've ever seen her this serious, and that's when it starts to sink in that this celebration could be really upsetting my grandfather.

'If you've gone against what I said, Ophelia...' My grandfather's voice cracks slightly as he composes himself. Melanie puts a hand on his arm.

'I... I said that—' My words tangle.

'Ophelia, we know how much you wanted to celebrate your birthday,' Melanie cuts in, her tone uncharacteristically harsh. 'But you've got to understand that this setting, after everything that happened, is just not appropriate.'

'And the way it was all carried out...' my grandfather adds. 'You knew Melanie and I had been away. We only got back yesterday. Then going through the post this morning, how do you think we felt when we opened that invite? By then it was too late, we only just made it this evening.'

'Had you planned that timing?' Melanie shoots the question at me, her eyes glued to mine, searching for the truth.

'No,' I shoot back, unblinking.

'Well, we can't stay… It's just too difficult. Especially after seeing that ambulance, you have no idea what it was like that night, Ophelia. My only son is gone.'

My grandfather's eyes are watering. I've never heard him speak about my dad with such emotion before. Perhaps that's why he doesn't talk about him. Maybe it's just too hard for him.

'We're going to go,' Melanie says abruptly.

'Go? But it's still early, won't you—'

'No, Ophelia. Not even for you. It's bringing it all back. I said under no circumstances should there be a party here, I know this house legally passes to you and your brother next week, as part of your inheritance when you both turn eighteen, but I would hope that you'd still respect my wishes. I will find out who is responsible for this and there will be consequences.'

With that, my grandfather gives me a curt nod and Melanie scurries after him. I'm left by myself, with tears welling in my eyes, wondering why they didn't believe me. It's funny because my grandfather is such an important person in my life but I only ever see him at snatched moments. Sometimes he's visited my boarding school but the majority of our meet ups are a day here or a weekend there when he has the time between his businesses and his holidays. And then I might not see him for weeks on end. We're usually surrounded by others when we do see each other so I always feel like I'm fighting for his attention, trying to get him to notice me. Tonight, he didn't give me the chance to defend myself and I'm upset he won't even stay to see me cut the cake or have one dance with me.

Brushing a stray tear from my cheek, I startle as Melanie appears in front of me once more. She clutches me to her tightly and whispers urgently, 'I'm sorry. This has unnerved Hugo more than you can imagine.'

She looks me full in the face and briefly touches my arm. 'We've got an early flight tomorrow. You know we were only staying in the UK for a night after staying with our friends in Jersey last month. We're heading to America to see your brother and then we'll see you in New York as planned for your actual birthday next week. We'll celebrate with you then.'

I bob my head up and down, holding back a sob, upset they won't stay for the rest of the evening.

'Enjoy the evening, don't let this spoil it. It's done,' she waves her hand around. 'I'm sure it was organised with good intentions. Have fun – and please don't hold this against Hugo. It's just a bit too much for him.'

Smiling weakly at her, I tell her I'll see her stateside next week. She gives me a small wave goodbye and then disappears into the throng of people clustered in front of the food trucks. The sun is beginning to set and the sky is an impressive combination of pinks and oranges. The pretty skyline and the warm weather couldn't be more perfect but instead of being excited about this I'm starting to feel a bit flat.

Seeing Anne-Marie hurt put a big dent in my mood and the conversation with my grandfather and Melanie has just killed any remaining enthusiasm I had. This was not how I was expecting my eighteenth celebration to turn out and I'm beginning to wish this event hadn't happened after all.

'Are you OK, love?' my grandmother Nadia asks, winding her arm around my waist. 'I overheard what Hugo said.'

Pulling away from her, I flick my hair over my shoulder and twitch my nose. 'Umm, yeah. It wasn't a great conversation. They're leaving.'

Nadia reaches towards me and squeezes my shoulder. 'It's not because of you, it's because of what happened to your father.'

'I do understand. Everyone thinks I'm too young, but I have feelings too.'

'I know you do... So Hugo and Melanie didn't arrange all of this then?'

'Nope,' I confirm. 'I thought it might've been Melanie, but apparently not.'

'Things will sort themselves out, Hugo loves you so much.'

'I just want our lives to be normal. Who else has to go through all this drama when a party is held at their house?'

Nadia smiles sadly. 'Your parents and what happened to them will always be a part of you, of your story, but we can move forward positively. And this is a big milestone for you. It's not every week you turn eighteen.'

I huff. 'Well, it doesn't feel like a celebration.'

'Come on, less of that. Let's get you back into the party.'

'What's that?' My aunt Leah joins us, brandishing a bottle of beer in one hand and an oversized burger in the other. 'Does someone need a drink?'

She winks and hands me her bottle of beer.

'Leah!' Nadia says in mock horror.

'She's almost eighteen, it's her birthday. Go on Ophelia.'

I grab the bottle from Leah and take a long swig of the lukewarm liquid.

Leah has always been the 'cool aunt', whisking me off for days out in London whenever she has some time free from her busy career. Sasha is the sensible aunt, the person who's been at the other end of the phone line whenever I've needed her. I should be grateful to them all, these Bailey women who flock round me when I need support and cheering up – just like now. Except, since I've been delving into the truth about my family's past, it's made me question the actions of my aunts and my grandmother. Lately, I've become aware that more than one of them have secrets that they're keeping from me.

It's hard to know where to begin unravelling the truth when my family's lies are so twisted up but, now that I've started on this track, I can't let it rest until I understand how and why the women who I've trusted and been closest to have spun a web of secrets and lies around me while I've been growing up. There are certain things I'm determined to find out.

Passing back the bottle to Leah, I think about her successful life as a journalist. She travels all over the world chasing down stories and then typing them up as fast as she can, sending her words out into the ether, not really knowing how much they will affect others. I don't really know what I want to do with my life yet, but perhaps investigating my own family's history will give me a thirst for hunting down the truth and I'll become a journalist like Leah. Or maybe uncovering how stories can be manipulated will put me off going down that route. Because Leah makes out that she's relaxed and open, yet it annoys me that she's never told me how she got the scar on her temple, even when

I've asked her outright. That's something she refuses to share with me, and I want to know why.

'Get some food while you're here,' Nadia encourages. I can tell she wants to make sure my stomach is properly lined before I have any more alcohol.

I'm not going to argue about this and I quite fancy one of the chocolate crêpes. 'Sure,' I agree. 'Why don't you check out the Tarot reader?'

Nadia whips her head round and clocks the Tarot reader's wagon just behind us. 'Oh, I hadn't seen that,' she laughs. 'Have you been in?'

'Yes,' I nod, confirming that I went in and spoke with the Tarot reader earlier.

'Was she any good?' Nadia queries.

I think about the first tarot card – the Three of Cups. The card showed three women dancing, holding drinks above their heads. The card represents celebrations, gatherings, parties. An obvious one for the Tarot reader to begin with. I wasn't impressed. I'm familiar enough with the cards and their meanings – at boarding school a friend of mine went through a phase of reading tarot cards for the girls in our dorm. It was more interesting to me to memorise the potential meanings of the various cards than it was to memorise the coronation dates of every ancient King of England.

The Lovers card came next, although this could've been another good guess from the veiled woman. After all, doesn't every eighteen-year-old girl wish for romance? That card was followed by the Wheel of Fortune and the Queen of Coins. All cards that I'm sure lots of young women would want to see in their reading.

But then, as the woman opposite me continued placing the dog-eared cards down on the circular table, I became more intrigued. The Five of Cups was placed on a new row. Not what I was expecting, as it isn't a card that represents happiness or celebration. The Five of Cups suggests loss or tragedy, it's come up for me when I've messed around with a deck of tarot cards myself. The next card was the Ten of Swords. The dark image on the front caused me to bite my tongue. I watched at the woman sitting across the table from me, but her face was mostly hidden under her veil. She wouldn't have put that card down if she was just going for an entertaining, easy reading. If I remember rightly that card represents the end of something.

'The storm rages... A limit has been reached,' she'd muttered.

The Devil card was carefully placed down next to the Ten of Swords. I immediately wanted to ask questions: why this card? And who in my life did it represent? But my thoughts were interrupted by that awful scream. It seemed to echo all around the Tarot reader's wagon and I felt cold all over. I ran from the wagon, gulping down the fresh evening air and searching for the source of the noise – which led me to Anne-Marie.

I snap back to the present and answer Nadia. 'Yes, she was OK, you should give it a go.'

With that, I shrug and part ways with my maternal family and head towards a group of my friends sitting on the rattan chairs just past the food trucks. My brain is full of conflicting thoughts and my heart bursting with emotions. I need to sit and chill for a bit, to take in the events of the evening so far and to surround myself with the normality of my friends.

My need for the truth feels like it's going to bubble up to the surface and explode. But maybe tonight isn't the time to figure everything out. Maybe I should just ignore the things I've begun to uncover and try and forget about it all. Because I meant what I said earlier... I'd love for my family to just be normal. To not have the weight of the past hanging around our necks or the whispers and the rumours that have surrounded me for my whole life.

Except I know that will never be possible because there's still a lot of media interest in my mum and dad. Especially my beautiful, mysterious mum. It drives me mad to think that other people out there know more about the events of my parents' past than I do. That's one reason I set off on this path of discovering the truth.

I watch as Nadia makes her way towards the Tarot reader's wagon. I don't believe in magic, but I can't help but be curious about if the cards were right about this night being a new chapter for me.

I just hope it's a good one...

Chapter Eleven

Nadia

Climbing the rickety wooden steps of the Tarot reader's wagon, I wonder what on earth is possessing me to do this. I know Ophelia has recently been fascinated by Tarot; it's something I've heard her talking about to her friends on video calls, and I guess this is my way of showing an interest and trying to connect with my granddaughter. I wouldn't necessarily seek out a Tarot reading of my own accord but I still like to think I've got an open mind and there's always a first time for everything. Pulling aside the beaded curtains, I find myself in the gloomy interior.

'Hello,' I say, my greeting immediately swallowed in the darkness.

'Welcome my dear,' a gravelly voice responds, 'I wasn't expecting you.'

This strikes me as an odd thing for someone in the business of fortune telling to say. Surely, it's in her job description to pre-empt things? But I have very little knowledge of any of this so I don't say anything.

'Come, come, sit down,' the woman calls to me. A small side lamp switches on and helps my eyesight adjust to the dim interior of the wagon. I dodge past a few dreamcatchers hanging from the ceiling and lower myself down into an old wooden chair. The woman sitting opposite me is hard to make out; she has a veil across her face and jangly bracelets at her wrists. A voice in my head whispers this is all very staged and stereotypical, but I squash down my doubts and try to approach it without any preconceptions.

'This is my first reading,' I say hesitantly.

'I know,' the woman replies.

I shift in the chair, unsure as to what will happen next.

'You are a mother, yes?' The question is asked but she doesn't wait for an answer. 'And you are worried?'

Exhaling, I agree with both questions asked of me. Being a mother and being worried come hand in hand but can this Tarot reader detect the extent of my fears? Does she really have any insight into my pain as a parent, or the troubles my children have been through?

'Why are you here? What is it you want to know?' the woman asks in a soothing tone.

I answer the first part honestly. 'My granddaughter suggested I give this a try.' The second question is more difficult – where do I begin with trying to put into words the one thing I'd like an answer to? Can I trust this stranger with my deepest fears?

Slowly, I respond, 'I want to know what's in store for my daughters.' This is the truth: if I had a crystal ball – like the woman sitting before me – and I had the knowledge that my children were going to live out the rest of their days happily and healthily then I'd be content. Although what I most want to find out is if this woman can tell me anything about my middle daughter. Can she give me any information about Erin? Does she know if my daughter is alive or dead?

The woman nods and begins shuffling a set of worn cards. I gulp, there's an incense stick burning in the corner and the musky scent hangs heavily in the air. My throat is scratchy but I ignore it and try to concentrate on the cards the woman is starting to press down on the table.

I have no idea what the different pictures mean or how they are going to answer my questions but I'm curious about what will happen next. Silence stretches across the room as more cards continue to be arranged on the table. My thoughts are filled with Erin, what she'd look like now, what she might be doing if she was still alive somewhere.

'Strength,' the woman says, pointing at the picture of a lion. 'You've proven your strength as a mother, bringing up your daughters and dealing with their problems.'

Nodding agreement, I listen intently as a few further cards are explained but all of them are supposed to represent things about me. She hasn't really mentioned my daughters yet and I begin to think my question has been forgotten.

And then, one by one, she points to cards and accurately describes each of my three children in turn. She lays down the Queen of Pentacles for my eldest daughter, describing Sasha as nurturing, capable and stable. The mystery woman even pinpoints that Sasha is a teacher and the archetype of the working mother. Everything she says matches with my daughter's personality and life.

Next, she puts down the Queen of Wands. She describes a woman who is bold and outgoing. As she goes on, I try to work out if she's referring to Erin or Leah. She describes a social butterfly and someone who is confident, which could again be either of them. It's when she starts talking about creativity and flair that I realise the Queen of Wands is Leah.

Nervously, I spin the bracelet round on my wrist. I hope she will lay down a card for Erin next. Or perhaps if she senses that Erin is no longer in this world then she wouldn't do that? A third card goes down, it's the Queen of Swords, but it's upside down.

'What does that mean?' I ask. 'It doesn't mean she's dead, does it?'

The Tarot reader gives nothing away. 'The cards just show personalities. I'm not getting a sense that your daughter has passed on.'

I exhale. Who knows if this woman is making things up as she goes along or connecting with some invisibly tapestry in the world. I cling to her sentence. 'Go on,' I urge her.

'The card is in reverse because this points to different aspects of a person's personality. In this case, the person is an intellect, a quick thinker, but the upside-down positioning of the card suggests that they are letting their heart rule their head. And therefore behaving negatively.'

I'm stunned. She's highlighted my daughters' different personalities as clearly as if she's met them, their flaws and their strengths all rolled into one. I sit back in the uncomfortable chair, my scepticism falling away.

Mouth gaping a little, I want to ask her how she knows all of this but she doesn't pause and presses on with a focus on the future. She tells me there are several Major Arcana cards that indicate big life changes. This is the crunch point, what I came in here for. But is it better to have a glimpse of the future or remain in blissful ignorance?

The Tower card shows a beautifully drawn princess-like tower but, when I peer closer, I can see lightning striking the top of the tower, flames licking the windows and what appear to be two figures falling through the air. I blink to clear my vision; I don't have my glasses to hand but the more I study the card the more I see – and the less I like.

'What does this mean?' I ask, an uncertain note creeping into my words.

'Change. For you and your daughters. And you'll be at the heart of that change.'

My shoulders slump; I've had enough change to last me an eternity. I was hoping the next phase of my life would be smooth and *unchanging* but according to this I've got more bumpy roads to navigate.

The remaining two cards don't seem like positive ones either – the darkness in the images tells me that before the mysterious woman speaks again.

'These two cards are often misunderstood. They're not necessarily meant to be read literally. This one,' she points a red-painted fingernail at one card, 'Is the Devil. And this one,' she points at the next, 'Is Death.'

'All good things then?' I try to joke, while internally telling myself that I'm lucky to have reached the age I'm at and not everyone gets to live to a hundred. 'Wait, are these cards showing what's next for me or for my daughters?'

'Your fate is tightly bound with that of your offspring,' she replies slowly.

'But is this my future or theirs? And this Death card, does that mean anything? Does that mean Erin is no longer alive?'

My head is spinning with possibilities and suddenly an overwhelming wave of emotion crashes over me. I just want to know what happened to Erin – the not knowing is agonising, and for a brief moment, I'd hoped this person could give me the answers I long for.

'The Tower card,' the woman points to it again. 'This is the strongest. It's calling out to me the most.'

As she leans forward, I glimpse strands of red hair under her dark veil. My heart is in my mouth. Seeing the flash of red hair has made every fibre of me focus intently on the person across the table from me. Could this woman know so much because she has some kind of connection to our family... Could this even be my missing daughter? I can't help myself; I lean forward and pull aside the veil. The woman instantly reels backwards.

'What are you doing?' she cries.

Red hair, pale skin, freckles so similar... And yet so different. The questioning brown eyes and oval shape of her face tells me all I need to know. It was a moment of madness. Of course this isn't my Erin.

'Sorry, I-I'm sorry,' I'm stuttering once more. 'I thought you might've been my daughter.' This used to happen a lot in the aftermath of Erin's disappearance, I'd see a face in a crowd and be convinced it was her, only to be wrong.

The charged atmosphere between us immediately softens. 'No, not me. But don't stop looking.'

My head jerks up and I stare at her hopefully. Does she have some kind of sixth-sense insight into Erin's disappearance? Can she tell me more?

Quickly and deftly, the woman begins stacking the cards. But she's building them up like a house, not packing them away. I watch, mesmerised, wondering what secrets will be unveiled. Just as she completes the structure, something buckles and the house of cards folds quickly and suddenly, scattering cards across the table. They all land face down, except for one – the Tower card.

The woman shakes her head. She looks at me and then beyond, towards the door. Rising abruptly, she rasps, 'I must go! I can't be here!'

'I don't understand?' I question. 'What happened, what does that mean?'

She's shaking her head, no longer willing to engage. 'I have to leave. It's time.' She shoos me away with her hands and I hurriedly get up from my seat. There's nothing left to say or do but follow her wishes. I move towards the door of the wagon and, as I go through the beaded curtain, I'm sure I can hear her voice whispering one sentence over and over again.

'Be careful. Be careful.'

Chapter Twelve

Ophelia

Throwing myself into a spare seat next to my friends, I smile impishly at them and hope they'll draw me out of my dark imaginings with their banter. Although, even as I start speaking, the Ten of Swords card flashes up in my mind once more.

Snatching the bottle being passed around, I take a deep swig of the bitter-tasting liquid and the scowl on my face deepens. My friends Lena, Taylor and Harper all seem to be obsessed with what happened to Anne-Marie. Only Lena got a glimpse of what was going on, but they're all talking about the event like it's an episode of one of our favourite reality shows. Lena is convinced there was something going on between Anne-Marie and one of the men who helped her into the ambulance.

'Maybe she's involved in some kind of juicy love triangle that she hasn't told us about?' Lena insists, her eyes lighting up at the idea.

I scoff, 'How? When? She'd barely been here for a few hours.'

Lena winks cheekily, 'That doesn't mean it couldn't have happened.'

'Urgh, those guys are old family friends – people who do business with my grandfather.'

'Maybe Anne-Marie was searching for a sugar daddy, she's so glam and I'm sure she'd—'

'No, just stop Lena! You're totally on the wrong track.'

Lena rolls her eyes at me. 'It's the only entertainment we've had so far at this lame party, let us have some fun, Ophelia.'

Taylor chokes back a laugh. It hits me that both Taylor and Harper agree with Lena, they all think this evening is lame. I don't blame them. The DJ is playing old, cheesy crowd-pleasers, none of the stuff we listen to. The fire-eater and the magician who's been weaving between groups and showing off tricks that a ten-year-old could do are so embarrassing.

'Let's take some selfies,' Harper suggests. 'Over there in that seating area.'

I give my friend a small smile and appreciate that she's trying to turn things around.

Lena rolls her eyes again. 'It's not quite the vibe I want on my platforms.'

'Lena, just do it, smile and have another drink.' Harper pulls Lena to her feet and we all follow her instructions. We arrange ourselves in different poses and experiment with the lighting on offer in an attempt to get the best photos we can, giggling in between pouting for the camera.

'Done!' Harper exclaims. 'This one of us all is gorgeous.'

'Shall we hit the dance floor then, see if there's any talent here even if the music is poor?' Lena says, making herself the centre of attention once again.

She's trying to bait me, to get me to react to her spiteful comments. Lena is often like this with me, we've always had a bit of rivalry, but you'd think she'd give me a break today of all days.

The other three link arms and head towards the main room. I follow them, my pink dress swishing through the grass. I feel alone without Jasper, I'm used to him being around and it's been weird these last six months not having him by my side – or even in the same country. And Lena has done a good job of continuing to wind me up while I've been feeling vulnerable. I swear she's trying to cut me out of our friendship group, she's always arranging things with Harper and Taylor when she knows I'm busy.

As we enter the room, the cheesiest pop song comes on and I cringe. Why, oh why did the DJ have to play this? Lena is raising her eyebrows and laughing. Instead of going to the dance floor, where a few women are bopping around their handbags, my friends head for the indoor bar.

I think about going over to the DJ booth and requesting some tunes that I know my friends will like. But there's no way I can do that subtly, and I'm sure Lena will only find a way to make fun of me if I do so. Then I have an idea.

'Lena, why don't you go and tell the DJ to put some proper music on. I'm sure you could persuade him.'

Lena appears unimpressed with this. 'If I have to go and request the music then this evening really is a mess.' She laughs cattily. Neither Taylor nor Harper respond, both of them looking uncomfortable.

'I'm done with this party, actually,' Lena says, loudly and clearly. 'It's still early and this obviously isn't going to pick up, let's go to a nightclub instead.' She smiles at Taylor and Harper.

This is it. This is the moment Lena has been working towards, elbowing me out of this friendship group and she's chosen my birthday to do it.

'We've got our IDs, so what are we waiting for?' Lena giggles, as though what she's suggesting isn't about to shatter my night. Lena, Taylor and Harper are all eighteen already. I'll be the last one to get my ID next week, so Lena knows I can't go with them – even if I did decide to exit my own celebration.

Digging my fingernails into my palms, I hope Taylor and Harper aren't going to bail on me tonight. I've been friends with these girls since we were all tiny. They're my boarding school family. They're not really going to just dump me at Lena's say-so, are they?

'Let's do it!' Taylor agrees. Lena's face brightens with glee. She knows she's won.

'Why don't you come with us,' Harper says to me. 'I'm sure we can get you in, you're only a week off your eighteenth.' I know she's trying to be the peacemaker; she's trying to include me even though it's clear Lena wants to cut me out.

'It's OK,' I say to Harper, giving her a quick hug. 'You go.'

My heart sinks as I watch my three friends slip away, linking arms once again as they leave my birthday party without a backwards glance. There are more clusters of my school friends here, but those girls are meant to be my besties. I can't believe they've just done that. And I know it won't be long before Lena is sending out messages to our other friends at the party, no doubt she'll be sharing photos of herself at whatever nightclub they get into and telling people to join her as well.

Pure rage boils inside me. There's nothing I can do though; Lena has finally taken my place in the group as alpha female, like when Cady Heron takes Regina George's crown in *Mean Girls*. I'd felt it coming and I should've done more to stop it. I should hang out with the remaining friends I have here, but I really don't know if I can face it. I find myself turning to the barman and asking for some prosecco. I've had a small glass of it on Christmas Day morning for the last few years and it's one of the few alcoholic drinks I actually like the taste of.

Knocking back the bubbles, I slip on my mask and head back outside. The sky is darkening and I'm hoping people will start getting into the party mood – perhaps things just kicked off a bit too early?

I try not to let my 'friends' bother me. After all, I've got other things to do tonight. I check my smartwatch and calculate how much time there is left. There are a few parts of my plan that I still need to sort out before I share my secret with my family. But I spy a group of people my age sitting around the fire pit and I make a beeline towards them. It won't hurt just to have one more drink first. I sit down on a bench positioned near to the flames and say 'hi' to the teenager sitting next to me.

I recognise some of the faces. Most of them are Freya's friends who I've bumped into at her house or at birthdays and hung around with during the school breaks when I've been at home. Although there are a few people here who I've never met before.

'Freya! Where've you been?' they ask me.

'Oh, she's bothered to come back,' another voice around the fire pit calls.

Pushing my mask off my face I laugh. 'Not Freya!' I put my hands up. 'I'm Ophelia – her cousin.'

'Ophelia – you guys are so alike, it's freaky.'

'Yeah, anyone would think you two are twins. You look more like her than Jasper.'

Laughing, I say, 'I'll take it as a compliment that you don't think I look like my brother.'

'Seriously, you two could swap places and I doubt any of us would be able to tell. If you hadn't said anything, I would've been chatting away to you with no idea it wasn't Freya.'

'I don't think we're that alike,' I reply.

'You are!' The response comes from a few different directions.

Freya's friends are more laid-back than my own. They're always laughing and joking around.

'She's gone off somewhere and left us anyway, so you can pretend to be Freya for us.'

Laughter rises up from several people sitting around the fire.

'Thanks,' I say with a note of sarcasm, although I'm wishing it was just that easy. That I could switch my life for Freya's, and my friends for hers. That would solve my current trashed social status. Besides, Freya always seems to have more luck than me in most things. Her mum's still alive, she still gets to live with her brother, and she's somehow managed to bag herself a super-hot boyfriend. Maybe pretending to be Freya for an evening wouldn't be so bad.

'Ha! I've got a great prank,' a guy in a beanie hat sitting nearby says. All heads swivel towards him. He tosses over Freya's denim jacket. I shrug it on, feeling slightly chilly and therefore grateful for the warmth but also wondering where this is going.

'Ophelia, you've got to do it! You've convinced us, let's see if you can convince Levi.'

'Convince Levi?' I repeat, trying to absorb what he means.

'Yeah, I bet you'd be able to pull the wool over his eyes too.'

'You bet?' another guy in the group asks.

A few others jump in and I find myself in the middle of a betting war even though I've agreed to nothing.

'This is ridiculous,' another person says.

'Hey,' I say. 'I haven't said yes yet. Why should I, what do I get out of this?'

'I'm sure we'll think of something,' the guy in the beanie hat says with a wink.

'Quick, he's coming!' A girl I know is called Pixie announces this in a stage-whisper.

A few of the other girls walk away, showing they don't agree or want any part in this. I should do the same and follow them. Except I don't want to be a social failure twice in one night, so I let my hair fall around my face and button up the denim jacket. Arranging myself on one of the wooden seats, I quickly grab an abandoned suit jacket and fling it over my lap so the striking colour of my pink dress can't really be seen. Then I pull the mask down over my face just as Levi shows up by the glowing fire.

He's tall and handsome, and completely head-over-heels for Freya. I know the moment I open my mouth he's going to hear my upper-class accent and immediately realise I'm not his girlfriend.

'Freya!' Levi exclaims. 'I've been searching for you everywhere.'

He's swaying a little and I'm guessing he's had a few drinks. I pause. I really shouldn't be doing this; it's a stupid prank and I shouldn't be getting myself involved. But there's a part of me that wants to step into Freya's shoes and to see what it would be like to have a boyfriend like

Levi. If I'm being honest with myself, I'm lonely. I'd love someone like Levi to pay me attention.

My heart beats faster as Levi moves closer to me. I'm aware that everyone else is watching us and there's a sense of expectation in the air. Before Levi has a chance to suss out the deception, I pull him towards me and kiss him.

A whoop goes up from the circle around us. I don't react because Levi is kissing me back. Kissing me like I've never been kissed before. One of his hands goes around my waist and the other in my hair, and I'm lost in the moment. The kiss deepens and the catcalls around us stop. Silence falls around us.

'Levi?'

Levi springs away from me, confused, before he sees Freya gaping at him. There's an expression of horror on her face. And then she clocks me.

My stomach flips.

'How could you?'

There's no chance to say anything because she's sprinting away from us; I can hear her crying already.

Emotions swirl around me, I feel guilty and ashamed. But the beanie hat guy is grinning at me with admiration and Levi still has his arms around me. He hasn't moved away from me yet. A part of me doesn't want him to.

Then I think about Freya. She's like a sister to me and I've just snogged her boyfriend.

Will she ever forgive me? Have I just ruined everything between us?

Chapter Thirteen

Sasha

'Yes, let's go ahead.' I glance at my watch and agree with the waitress who's sidled up to me to check if it's OK to bring the two cakes out for the obligatory blowing-out-of-candles and photo-taking moment.

'I'll bring two knives,' the waitress assures me, and then scurries off in the direction of the kitchen.

'It's nearly cake o'clock,' I say to Leah.

'Ooh yum, I'm ready for it,' Leah responds enthusiastically.

'Me three,' says Tiana, Leah's girlfriend of the last five years. They're standing next to each other, their shoulders touching.

'I'm so glad you made it tonight,' I say to Tiana. 'Mum will be thrilled to see you.'

Tiana meets my gaze. 'I'm sorry I was so late; a work thing, you know what it's like…'

Tiana is a journalist – it's how she and Leah met. They work for the same media outfit now and, although they're not part of the same team, sometimes their professional lives cross over at various industry events and celebrations. Leah is often liable to run a little behind because of a job she's assigned to but Tiana is notorious for being hours late – or a complete no-show.

The tension Leah was emitting earlier on is gone. I'm guessing she was worried about Tiana not showing up to this family gathering. Now her girlfriend is here, she is all smiles. Leah throws an arm around Tiana's shoulder at this point and plants a kiss on her cheek. I'm happy for Leah and I'm glad she has found someone to share her life with. I just hope that Tiana is as committed to Leah as Leah is to her. Because I've been in a relationship before where the other person wasn't all in, and it's not a nice feeling to be the one who's making all the effort and getting nothing back. Leah knows where I am if she needs me, and I don't want to meddle unnecessarily, but I make a mental note to organise a catch-up for just the two of us soon. She has such a fast-paced lifestyle and we don't check in with each other as much as we should.

'I'll go and get the birthday girls,' Leah tells me, and she and Tiana slope off to find them. Douglas joins me then, with a sleepy-eyed Fergus in his arms.

'He's getting tired,' Douglas says.

'We should think about getting him home,' I agree.

'Well, I can take him back; you and Freya can stay and enjoy the night.'

Douglas is always so thoughtful. 'I think I want to get back as well. I just need to persuade Freya.'

Douglas nods, recognising my desire to leave Burcott House. He understands me well enough and I know he'll step up and aim to get us home as soon as politely possible.

'After the cake comes out,' I suggest.

Before Douglas can answer, I notice a dishevelled Freya standing in the doorway. Her mascara is smudged and her hair is no longer sleek in the way she'd styled it earlier. Her chest is heaving and even from across the room I can tell she's upset.

'Freya?' I spring towards her.

'Mum!'

'What's the matter?' I fold her into my arms and feel her thin body heaving with emotion. All sorts of thoughts fly through my brain. 'Freya, tell me what's wrong.'

Freya glances between Douglas and me. I can tell she wants to talk to me privately and Douglas has picked up on this too. He gives me a reassuring smile and then moves away to give us some space.

My daughter steps out of my embrace, her bottom lip quivering just like it used to do when she was a child and had fallen over and scraped her knee. But I can tell that whatever's affected her is going to take longer to heal than a few cuts and bruises.

'It's Levi.'

'Levi? What's he done? Has he hurt you?'

'No... no.' Freya breaks into fresh sobs once more, and I draw her into a little alcove in the room, away from prying eyes.

Pushing a flyaway strand of auburn hair back from her face, I say, 'Freya, whatever it is, you can tell me.'

I feel her trembling once more until eventually she regains control of herself. 'I saw him kissing another girl.'

'Kissing...?' Part of me wants to sigh with relief. I know Freya will be devastated about this but my imagination had jumped to far worse conclusions.

'Oh honey, I'm sorry.' I hug my daughter close to me.

'He was kissing Ophelia.'

I groan internally. Levi kissing another girl was of course going to be upsetting for Freya, but I'm sure we could've navigated the fallout together and, after a few weeks of teenage heartbreak, Freya would have dusted herself down and moved on. But Levi kissing Ophelia? I see why Freya is distraught.

'Are you sure?' I ask gently.

She nods, appearing more miserable than I've ever seen her before.

'Right, well there's only one thing for it.' I raise Freya's chin and get her to properly focus on what I'm about to say. 'We're going to speak to them both and work out what on earth is going on. You deserve to know and we can only sort things out when we know the truth.'

I make sure I sound clear and confident, but inside I'm quaking. I've been in Freya's shoes before; I've been the person cheated on by two of the people I loved most in the world. I know how much this hurts. Erin did the same to me, and now Ophelia is following in her mother's footsteps. I can't bear it. How does this family keep making the same mistakes over and over again?

Adrenaline spikes within me and I grab Freya's hand. I'm ready to go and confront Ophelia and Levi to find out exactly what they were playing at, but before I can escape the warm room, I'm stopped in my tracks.

'Happy birthday to you, happy birthday to you...'

Oh no. This is now the worst possible time for the cake to come out.

Four waitresses move to the centre of the room, two of them clutching a pink cake with Ophelia emblazoned across it and the other two holding a royal-blue cake with my mother's name elegantly piped onto it.

Before I can whisk Freya out of the room, my mother enters from the garden. She's beaming and looking more comfortable with the attention than she did earlier. Ophelia follows her. Normally she'd be revelling in something like this but instead she's wide-eyed, her mouth set in a firm line with no hint of a smile. I notice she's wearing my daughter's denim jacket – does this have anything to do with the kiss Freya mentioned?

Our friends and family cluster closer and the two birthday girls take their places in the middle of the room. After the singing has stopped, my mother and niece both lean forward to blow out the candles burning brightly in front of them. My mother always says you should make a wish for the coming year when blowing out your birthday candles – it's a family tradition. The flames are extinguished. I wonder what my mother has wished for – and I'm even more curious to understand what Ophelia is thinking.

'Thank you, everyone!' my mother says.

'Speech! Speech! Speech!' The chant goes up from family and friends. Usually, Ophelia would step in and take over at a moment like this but she hesitates for a beat.

I hold my breath, waiting to see how my niece will react. One thing is for sure, she's not behaving like her usual self.

Ophelia then smiles, although I can tell it's forced and not genuine, as she shouts, 'Let's eat cake!'

My eyes remain on her. Her celebration is over. I'm going to talk to my niece to find out what's been going on. Freya and Ophelia have had such a close relationship growing up, so why has Ophelia chosen to betray her cousin? What's going on between Ophelia and Levi?

And is history about to repeat itself...?

Chapter Fourteen
Ophelia

This party is a complete disaster. First my friends abandoned the celebration for a better offer, and I've made things even worse by kissing my cousin's boyfriend. I don't know what to do. A waitress shoves a flimsy paper plate with a thick wedge of chocolate cake on it into my hands. I'm not hungry and the idea of the gooey icing sticking in my throat makes me want to gag. I clutch hold of the plate anyway, my eyes fixed on the cake while I try to sort out my thoughts.

There's only one thing I can do – apologise to Freya.

I swallow down my pride and look up. I spot my aunt Sasha immediately; her attention is fixed on me. Her eyes are slightly narrowed – she knows what I've done. My stomach clenches. This is going to be worse than I imagined. Sasha is a headteacher and it's a job she's well suited to. She's always made her expectations about behaviour clear and, for the most part, I've toed the line she's set. I've always been grateful for how much effort Sasha has made to be involved in my life and I've tried to be a good niece in return. I've totally blown that now.

Placing down the plate and pulling off Freya's denim jacket, I move towards Sasha. It's only then that I see Freya is hovering just behind my aunt.

'Freya, let me explain—'

'What is there to explain?' Freya fires back at me, before I've even finished my sentence.

I feel terrible. How could I let myself get drawn into a prank like that, when Freya's feelings were at stake?

'I'm sorry. It was stupid of me. A stupid, stupid mistake.'

'You were kissing my boyfriend! How do you make a mistake like that?' Teardrops are rolling down Freya's face, I've never seen her this upset.

'It was a prank. The others egged me on. I shouldn't have done it. And Levi didn't know, he thought I was you.'

'A prank? Why would you do that?'

'I... I want to tell you, but can we just calm down?'

'Calm down? If this was the other way round, you'd be screaming at me!'

Freya's words are coming at me through clenched teeth. She's right, if she'd done this to me it's very likely I'd be letting rip at her.

'I know. I'm in the wrong. Levi didn't have anything to do with it.' I offer her the denim jacket back. 'I put this on...'

Freya snatches the jacket out of my hands.

'Freya, I didn't mean it—'

'I don't want to hear any more. Leave me alone!'

Freya whips around and makes a quick exit through the doors leading to the entrance of the hotel.

My eyes fill with emotion.

'She has every right to be cross with you,' Sasha says to me firmly. 'I don't know what happened out there, but you have some making up to do.'

Sasha's arms are crossed and she makes it clear she has no sympathy for me.

My aunt then stalks away in the same direction as Freya. Very quickly my sadness turns to anger. Sasha and Freya didn't even acknowledge the fact I was sorry or listen to my side of the story. I know I did something stupid and I've hurt her. But Sasha didn't even try and listen to me. She didn't even ask me if there was something more to it. That just proves once and for all that she will always choose Freya over me. Sasha says she's my surrogate mother but when it comes to it, she will pick Freya every time.

I throw myself down in a chair at the edge of the room and, as the minutes tick by, I get more worked up about the situation. Why couldn't my aunt and cousin just hear me out? I know I'm in the wrong but they've made me feel like I'm the worst person on earth. Frustrated thoughts swirl around my mind. Freya is lucky that she has a mother to comfort her. I'm sure she and Levi will patch things up as they're so into each other, and I doubt she's going to blame anyone in her friendship group for egging me on to kiss Levi. The only person who is going to come off badly from this is me.

It's just not fair... Freya has everything I don't have: a family unit, someone who adores her and a big group of friends. I don't have any of those things. I know that's not an excuse though – it's not her fault. Freya is also the only real friend I have. I don't have anyone else I can turn to now I've messed up.

I feel tears rising – I can't believe I did such a stupid thing.

'You were great out there.'

My head snaps up and I take in the beanie hat guy standing in front of me.

'Go away,' I snap at him at him, folding my arms across my chest.

'Oh, come on.' He smiles broadly at me. 'It was just a joke.'

'I shouldn't have done it,' I mumble.

'It was only a laugh,' he replies, still smiling.

'Try telling Freya that.'

'Has she gone off in a huff? She's always so uptight.'

'A bit more than a huff.'

'If it helps, Levi is mad at me too.'

'At you?'

'Yeah, one of the girls grassed me up, told him it was my idea. I'm always in trouble; I'm used to it. Do you want me to go tell Freya it was all on me?'

Dragging my hands through my hair, I'm seriously tempted to say yes. But he doesn't need to shoulder all the blame. I didn't have to go along with his suggestion.

'What's your name?' I ask.

'Toby.' Toby is nothing like Levi, who is tall and blond with model looks. Toby is shorter, only a few inches taller than me, and stockier than Levi. Along with the beanie hat, Toby has a stud in his eyebrow and stubble along his jaw. He's got a mischievous twinkle in his green eyes that makes me believe that he really is always in trouble.

'Well Toby, I think we both need another drink.' Even though he's the reason Freya and I have fallen out, there's something about him that's drawing me to him. He's not stereotypically attractive, but he's full of confidence – and cheeky with it – that I'm curious to find out more about him. And besides, everyone is mad at us so it's not like we have anyone else to talk to.

Grinning at me, Toby takes my hand into his larger, warmer one. Instantly, my stomach feels like it's been filled with butterflies. As we make our way towards the bar area, I hope this evening is going to get more interesting after all...

Toby orders two beers. I'm aware I'm mixing my drinks but having a headache tomorrow morning is the least of my worries. I gulp down the liquid and try not to grimace at the bitter taste. Toby slings an arm around my shoulders and we weave through the guests clustering in the bar area.

Outwardly, I'm talking and laughing like nothing is wrong but, on the inside, I'm still simmering with anger. I wish Freya and Sasha had listened to me.

Since Mum disappeared, Sasha has behaved like the martyr who's taken her sister's child under her wing, but she didn't even pause to try to understand what was going on with me. If she did, maybe I would've told her how lonely I've been feeling without Jasper and mentioned the problems in my friendship group and how it all came to a head tonight. Instead, I feel more on my own than I ever did and it's becoming clear that Sasha only pretends to be my mother when it's convenient for her.

I would do anything to have a proper family of my own again, instead of the patchwork alternative I have. Everything has changed in the last few months. But I'm going to take control of my own life and do the things that I want to do. I'm determined not to be the victim of my family's tragic past anymore.

From now on, things are going to be different.

Chapter Fifteen

Nadia

The DJ is announcing that the masquerade ball is about to begin. There's a flurry of activity as guests slide on their masks. The effect is quite something as the familiar faces around me instantly transform into an array of intricate masks that completely change the appearance of the people I know. The combination of the free-flowing alcohol and the masks makes my head spin a little.

A frisson of excitement shoots through me. I've always wanted to go to a masquerade ball and now here I am. The glamour, the dresses, the dancing: it's all so enchanting. I slip my own mask on and then cast around for my granddaughter, searching the room for her bright pink dress. I want to see her joy in this moment too but there are lots of people in the room and I can't see her. A few more plus-ones and evening guests have arrived by this point. But who has invited them? It's still bothering me that I don't know who's organised this party.

Whoever is responsible has done an exceptionally good job of keeping it a secret. I run through the list of possibilities. Sasha and Leah have both said they weren't involved in the party and I believe them. Ophelia has denied knowing about it, and judging by the reaction from Hugo and Melanie, a party at Burcott House was the last thing they wanted.

The next possibility is Jasper. He knew how much Ophelia wanted a big birthday celebration, perhaps he's planned this from afar? A gift to his sister while he's out of the country? It would be out of character for him to be really proactive with setting something like this up but maybe I'm underestimating my grandson. He's about to turn eighteen too and he's more than capable of sending out invites and booking entertainment. I make a mental note to send him a text this evening to check. If it's not Jasper then I'll need to think again.

The music strikes up at the exact same point my excitement gives way to a burst of panic. The embellished masks are making it hard to tell who is who, and I feel overwhelmed looking across the room at the half-obscured faces. For the whole evening, I've been on high alert, watching to see if the party has attracted any unwanted guests, and now that is much harder to do.

The Bailey family still gets a certain level of interest from the general public and from the media. I haven't seen any kind of security here this evening and that worries me. It's not out of the realms of possibility that a journalist or a particularly enthusiastic true crime fan will have got wind of this celebration. After all, party invites have been sent out and you never know which guests may have unwittingly – or deliberately – passed on the details to an interested source. I try to tell myself it's unlikely, as the media circus around our family has reduced in recent years, but it's still a niggling thought.

A few of the entertainers, previously in leotards but now wearing ballgowns and suits, are on the stage and encouraging everyone to follow their dance steps. This is going to be entertaining, that's for sure. A man, wearing a dark blue suit and a blue mask that almost matches the colour of my own, steps towards me.

'May I have this dance?' He gives a little bow and I laugh.

'It would be my pleasure,' I respond, in the most formal tone I can muster.

He takes one of my hands in his and places the other hand around my waist. We both turn slightly to follow the dancers on the stage. After a couple of stumbles, I get the hang of the simple steps and begin to get into a rhythm.

'Thank you for coming tonight, Gareth,' I say, my mouth close to his ear because of the way we're dancing.

'I wouldn't have missed it for the world.'

Gareth is one of the members of my ski group. He's a widower and we've known each other for a while. The pair of us have always got on well and, lately, we're spending more and more time together at the social events put on by the ski club. He's an attractive man with old-fashioned manners – and great company. I like him a lot. None of my previous relationships have ended well, so I've been keeping him at arm's length. I don't want to get involved with him and then have our friendship ruined.

I blow out a breath.

'Penny for your thoughts?' Gareth asks, as the music ends.

'There's no need for me to bore you,' I chuckle, brushing off his inquiry.

'Go on, try me,' Gareth insists.

The music begins again and the dancers on the stage begin a different routine. 'We'd best concentrate, otherwise one of us will end up with a broken toe!'

Successfully deflecting his interest once more, I go back to following the steps to the music and he follows suit. While this isn't quite as smooth or effortless as the dances I've watched on the telly, it's still thrilling to actually be doing this. And I'm content to keep my relationship with Gareth as it is – after all, my first love ended up in prison and the second man I fell for died in a horrible car crash. I can't risk breaking my heart like that again. And what if I somehow hurt my wonderful friend?

I allow the music to wash over me and enjoy the experience of dancing. There's still no sign of Ophelia – it's pretty hard to work out who is who with all these masks on but her pink dress is so distinctive that it would be hard to miss it. I don't want her to miss out on all of this. I haven't seen Sasha or Freya lately either. Although dancing like this isn't really Sasha's kind of thing, I wouldn't be surprised if she's extracted herself from the room and gone in search of somewhere comfortable to sit.

'Having fun?' Gareth asks.

'Yes.' I nod. 'You?'

'I'm having the best night.'

I let the sentence hang in the air because I don't want to break the spell between us. I rest my head on his shoulder and think about how incredible it could be if I allowed myself to open up to this kind and honest man.

In a split second, the moment is broken.

'Grandmother!'

The voice sounds urgent and panicked. I step out of Gareth's arms to find a flushed Ophelia in front of me. From the look on her face, I know she's angry.

'Ophelia, what's wrong?'

She glances between Gareth and I before rolling her eyes. I reach out to catch my granddaughter's arm but she jerks out of my grasp.

'Oh, forget it!' She storms.

I watch her burst out of the oak doors of the Winchester Room and catch a glimpse of her pink dress swirling around her legs as she runs down the corridor. I wonder what on earth has shaken her. I should go after Ophelia but I'm certain she's just having one of her dramatic moments.

I look back in the direction Ophelia came from and notice that a teenager in a beanie hat is standing in my granddaughter's wake, appearing bemused.

I head over to him. 'Do you know why Ophelia is upset?'

He shrugs his shoulders and makes a grunting noise, in the way that only teenage boys know how to do.

'Were you with her?'

His head bobs up and down in response.

'Did you argue?' I press – it's like getting blood from a stone talking to him.

'No,' he says forcefully. 'It was her, she started yelling at me... she's crazy!'

My mouth gapes open a little. Ophelia can be hot headed with her family at times but I didn't realise she behaved the same way with her friends. The question is, what has she been arguing about now?

Before I can ask anything more, the boy stalks off. He's clearly eager for an escape.

'Is everything OK?' Gareth is at my side, full of concern.

'I hope so Gareth. I really hope so...'

Chapter Sixteen

Sasha

'How could she do it?' Freya is sitting on a squishy sofa in the snug, with tears still spilling down her face.

I pass her another tissue. 'I don't know, sweetheart,' I say honestly. 'Sometimes people do things and you feel like you'll never understand why they behaved in the way they did.'

Freya sniffs and wipes her eyes with the tissue. 'She's like a sister to me. I trusted her.'

Putting an arm around my daughter, I give her a reassuring squeeze. 'For what it's worth, I really don't think she thought things through. Knowing Ophelia, she acted on impulse. And she'd been drinking too.'

'That's no excuse!'

'You're right, I'm not trying to make excuses for her but I am trying to put things into perspective. I don't think Ophelia meant to betray you like that.'

'Is this what it was like for you?' Freya cocks her head as she waits for me to speak.

'What what was like?' I ask her, pretty sure I know what she means, but stalling having to answer.

'How did you feel? When you found out about my dad cheating on you?'

Hesitating, I try to choose my words carefully. I always knew my daughter might ask this question so I've thought about it a lot. I just didn't expect it to come tonight while we're back here, at Burcott House, the place where I discovered that Jesse was not only a cheat but a murderer too.

'It's hard to describe... but apart from feeling angry and sad and hurt the main feeling that stayed with me for months was this sense of being really disorientated. It was like someone was shaking me up and down and throwing all the elements of my life up in the air. It was hard, I struggled for a long while. I believed I'd never be happy again.'

Freya appears a little stunned by my honesty, but I vowed to tell her the truth if we ever had this conversation. Maybe talking about this will stop her making the same mistakes I did.

'You got me through.' The tears are pooling in my eyes. 'I got up and I kept carrying on for you.'

Rubbing my temples, I pause and then say, 'It was the worst period of my life but I wouldn't change it because it made me who I am today. And if I hadn't been through all that, I would never have met Douglas or had your brother.'

'You don't regret being with my dad then?' Freya asks quietly.

'No!' I clasp her hands tightly in mine. 'Because we did love each other once. I wish things had turned out differently but the main thing is we had you. Whatever we've done, both me and your father love you very much.'

Freya sinks into my arms once more and I can feel the silent sobs as her ribs move up and down. It hasn't been easy, but I've never stopped

Freya from being in contact with Jesse. Yes, he did the worst thing a human being can do but I do believe it was a crime of passion and that he wouldn't repeat it.

I stroke Freya's hair in an attempt to soothe her. I know how much Jesse loves our daughter and how hard he has found being apart from her. I also know how much she loves him. Freya and Jesse write to each other on a weekly basis, they have occasional phone calls and she visits him in prison every other month. It's not the kind of father and daughter relationship I'd imagined, but it's teaching Freya valuable life lessons. She fully realises there are consequences to every action, which is how I know she's going to struggle with what Ophelia and Levi have done.

'I'm sorry, Mum,' Freya squeaks.

'Sorry? Why?'

'I shouldn't have compared Levi kissing someone to what you went through with Dad. I was just...'

'It's OK, I understand.' I sigh deeply. 'The thing I've learnt is that you can't predict or control other people's actions. You can only be responsible for yourself, and you should never, ever, blame yourself for other people's actions. That way madness lies...'

Freya hugs me a bit tighter and I know that she understands, despite her inexperience. She may not remember all of it but she was there when I was at my lowest. She's got an old head on young shoulders and she's not far off becoming an adult herself. I'm not going to hide things from her, because keeping secrets is the main reason why our family has had so many problems.

We sit together a little longer. The warmth of the fire and the flames dancing in the grate are soothing. Even though it's summer it's getting cooler as the evening wears on and these big airy houses always get cold so the fire at this point is very welcome. My head tips back and I could very easily fall asleep right here. It's not even ten o'clock yet but because the party started early it feels much later.

'Sasha? Sasha?'

I jerk upright at the sound of Douglas's voice and stare at my husband. Panic is etched across his face, but why?

'What's wrong?' I ask.

'Have you seen Fergus?'

'Fergus? He was with you?'

Douglas rubs his jaw agitatedly. 'He was, he fell asleep. I put him down on that chaise longue in the hallway, I thought it would be quieter there for him. I was checking back and forth – he's been fast asleep. But I just went to check on him again and he's gone.'

'Gone? He must be here somewhere.' I get up, the practical side of my brain kicking in. Fergus has been asleep in the house. If he's woken up then he's bound to be somewhere inside.

'I've been looking everywhere for the last five minutes.'

'How long since you last saw him?'

'I checked him about fifteen, maybe twenty minutes before that and he was in a deep sleep.'

Almost half an hour feels like too long for Fergus not to be accounted for.

Douglas is pacing up and down; he looks frantic. A wave of panic crashes over me. Fergus can't have gone far; we just have to search properly. I can't help feeling terrified all of a sudden but I need to keep a clear head. I place my hands on my husband's shoulders and get him to stand still.

'Stop. Breathe. We're going to find him.'

Douglas calms a little.

'Mum, Fergus isn't really lost, is he?' Freya asks, she's gone as white as a sheet.

'Freya, he's wandered off somewhere so let's all go and find him. Can you go into the Winchester Room please and start there? And ask around to see if anyone has seen him.'

Freya does as I tell her. I link hands with Douglas and we go back to the hallway just off the grand foyer.

'He might have been half-asleep and unsure of his surroundings. I've searched in all the downstairs rooms... I don't know why I haven't found him yet.'

'How long did you say it was since you last checked on him?'

'About twenty minutes ago.'

My heart hammers against my ribcage. That's not a long time, but it's too long for my child to be unaccounted for. Fergus could be disorientated or scared, or he might have fallen and hurt himself.

'OK, he could've gone up the stairs, or into the garden.' We both stare up at the twisting, marble staircase. 'I doubt he would've gone up,' I say decisively.

'Freya has gone back into the main party room – I checked there first,' Douglas tells me, trying to match my steady tone but failing, his voice instead coming out uneven.

'This way.' We speed towards the reception area at the front of the building. I'm praying that we'll catch sight of Fergus's mop of red-brown hair.

'Oh no!' I exclaim. The front door to Burcott House is wide open. There are a few people around outside, smoking and chatting. In the darkness I see car headlights moving away and a few more people getting into other cars. Some of the guests are leaving the party already. My anxiety kicks up a gear.

Douglas groans beside me. 'He wouldn't have come out here, would he? Not without us?'

'Excuse me, excuse me!' I hurriedly address the group chatting by the door, wafts of cigarette smoke hitting my nostrils. 'Have you seen a little boy, about this high...' I gesture my son's height. 'Out here, in the last twenty minutes?'

A man in a crumpled cream shirt shrugs nonchalantly and I want to scream at him. My child has vanished and all he can do is shrug. A couple murmur between themselves but their eyes are glazed over and they both have bottles of beer in their hands. I don't think I could rely on their recollections anyway. Then a woman in high heels steps forward.

'I haven't seen a child.' She doesn't seem as though she's had much to drink and she's confident in her answer.

'Are you sure?'

'Certain. I've been out here for half an hour and no kids have come out. I've had my eye on the door in case my other half caught me having a cheeky smoke.' She laughs at this and then gives my shoulder a squeeze. 'What does he look like? We can help you find him.'

Words tumble out of my mouth as I describe my beautiful boy to this stranger. I'm filled with gratitude as she begins organising the handful of people milling around.

'We'll double check out here first, but you go in. I'm sure he'll be inside.'

I hesitate. My gut instinct is telling me to stop the cars pulling out of the car park and go and search them all to make sure Fergus hasn't crawled into the back of one of them – or worse, that no one has deliberately enticed him into a car. I think about the people attending this evening's celebrations: they're Ophelia and my mother's friends and family. I know many of them personally and not one of them would have a motive to take my little boy away from his parents, would they?

'You'll find him soon,' the woman reassures me with a kind smile. She seems trustworthy; I'm sure she's one of my mother's friends from her days working at the supermarket.

I cast my eyes around once more before thanking her and heading back into Burcott House with Douglas. We check the bathroom and the hallways downstairs but there's no sign of Fergus. Then we decide to split up. Douglas takes the stairs to do a search of the floors above us while I go and look in the garden.

My heart is thumping hard in my chest and my thoughts keep flying to all sorts of dreadful scenarios but I keep my focus. Fergus has just turned six, it's not like he's a toddler. He's at an age when he can do things for himself to a certain extent. My worry is that he doesn't have the best sense of direction. There've been a few incidents at school, including an occasion when he ended up in the wrong classroom at school pick-up and another when he wandered off during a school trip, which have worried me. Even though he's been to Burcott House many times before, it's such a sprawling building and he doesn't know it very well so he could easily have gotten confused in unfamiliar surroundings.

All these thoughts are whirring as I enter the Winchester Room. I scour the edges of the vast space first but I still can't see him. The majority of guests have their masks on, which makes it much harder for me to see who is in the room and who I can ask for help. My eyes land on a figure by one of the windows. There's something familiar about the way they're standing but the black silk mask is covering two-thirds of their face and I can't place who it is. It's unsettling.

'Have you found him?' My mother materialises in front of me, with Freya next to her.

'No, but I'm about to try the garden.'

'I'll come with you,' Freya says. We spread out and I make a beeline for the food trucks in case Fergus has decided he was hungry, but there's no sign of him.

'Have you seen a boy with red-brown hair, about this high?' I ask a group of teenagers who I recognise as Freya's friends. They all shake their heads casually, none of them noticing my concern.

Moving away from the clusters of groups chatting, I scour the trees in case he's decided to climb up any of them but he's nowhere to be seen. The light is fading fast and the evening is beginning to cool. I scrutinise the patio area outside Burcott House and then the lavender fields beyond. What if he's decided to go exploring? He keeps saying he wants to be an adventurer when he grows up. Could he have decided to venture out into the wider grounds of the hotel?

I don't even know how much land is attached to Burcott House, it's so vast. The flower fields have a path weaving through them which leads to the cottage that is Ophelia and Jasper's family home. But where does that path go to after that? There are woods beyond and then the little country village. Surely he wouldn't have gone that far?

Catching sight of Freya, I bolt over to her. 'Any luck?' I question.

'No,' she replies, unsmiling.

'You haven't found him either then?'

Shaking her head, Freya says, 'I feel really worried now.'

'Me too,' I agree.

I take my daughter's hand and we head back inside together. My mother is still in the Winchester Room; she takes one glance at my face and must realise how stressed I am.

I close my eyes briefly, unable to speak as the panic builds within me.

'Freya, get the DJ to stop the music and put an announcement out,' my mother orders.

Once again Freya obediently follows instructions. I can't stay here doing nothing, so I race to the other end of the room hoping to find Fergus by the chocolate fountain. But he's not there.

'Ladies and gentlemen, I'm going to stop the music for a bit. We're looking for a six-year-old boy called Fergus. Fergus, mate, if you're in the room let an adult know, or if someone has seen the little guy please come and let me know immediately.'

A hush descends over the room. No-one moves and there's no sign of my son. I feel sick with nerves.

'OK, in that case, folks, can everyone stay put for just a bit longer. If you can stand still rather than moving around too much that would be appreciated.'

'I'll go and search in the garden again,' Freya comes back to tell me. Mascara is still streaked around her eyes and she looks frightened.

'Where is he?' My voice cracks as I turn towards my mother.

'He'll be here somewhere. Don't you worry.' Although I can tell from the way she says this that she's just as worried as I am.

I glance at my watch; it's been almost an hour since Fergus was last seen. I just want to hold my baby in my arms. Where has he gone? This is such a big house. Is he just hiding somewhere? Has he had an accident?

This room is full of people and not one of them has put their hand up to say they've seen him. A lot of the guests are close friends and family but, as I gaze around at them, I realise there are more people that I don't recognise than I'd like – Ophelia's friends and family, as well as staff working at the hotel.

Suddenly, I'm overwhelmed with fear.

Has someone taken my son?

Chapter Seventeen

Nadia

Little Fergus is nowhere to be seen. I was convinced we'd discover him sleeping under a chair or sneaking food from one of the trucks outside but he's still not been found. The party has been called to a halt and I'm organising small search groups. I can't believe this is happening. It doesn't help that most people still have their masquerade masks on so trying to look around the room to see if there's anyone here who shouldn't be is made more difficult. I'm finding the number of people in the building, combined with their fancy outfits, and the level of noise disorientating. And the fact he hasn't been found yet is pushing my anxiety levels higher and higher.

I hope Fergus is just hiding behind a curtain and that one day in the future this will be a funny story that we tell.

The longer he is gone, the more I'm worried there could be something sinister going on. I still don't know who organised this surprise party. All evening I've been trying to find out who's behind it but I've got no clear idea of who put all of this together. I wish I'd tried harder to work it out. Because what if the party has been arranged with an ulterior motive in mind? It's been my fear since the moment everyone shouted 'Surprise!' What if someone else knew about why I'd come to the hotel today? If it was any other date, I would probably be less concerned but today's date is significant. Although surely no-one would go as far as taking a child as young as Fergus away from his family, even if they were out for revenge?

'Sorry everyone, I'm sure the cheeky thing will jump out of his hiding place and shout "Boo" at us all soon,' I bluster, trying to keep positive.

'Nadia,' my niece Hayley says to me. 'Everyone understands, we just want to find Fergus too.'

'I'll go with the group searching in the garden.' Andrew, Hayley's partner, heads off purposefully.

'It's just such a huge place,' I say to Hayley. 'He could be anywhere.'

She nods. 'I know but he won't have gone far. He's probably snoring his head off in one of the rooms.'

'You're right.' I can't go to pieces; I've been reassuring Sasha of the very same thing. Except, it's hard not to think the worst when you've already experienced the disappearance of a child. Erin was a fully grown woman when she went missing in the French Alps but that didn't make it any easier. The not knowing what happened to her still eats me up every single day and this situation is bringing it all flooding back.

'What a way to halt the party,' I try to joke.

'Don't worry about that, Fergus is the priority. I'm going to add another pair of eyes to the search.' Hayley gives me a reassuring squeeze before she goes.

I move back towards the snug; I want to have another check in the downstairs areas myself. I push the blue satin mask off my face so I can see better and enter the cosy room. It's a hive of activity, sofas have been pushed back, everything has been upturned in the search for Fergus.

'Ophelia!' I approach my granddaughter. 'No luck in here?' I ask.

'Not here. He will turn up.'

Ophelia sounds certain, but I'm becoming more worried that this might not be as simple as a six-year-old playing hide-and-seek.

'I'm sorry I was cross with you,' I say. Ophelia told me that she kissed Levi and I made it clear that I wasn't happy about her actions. We had a heated exchange but this just puts everything in perspective – how important she is to me, how important all the children in our family are.

Ophelia chews her lip; she looks exactly like her mother Erin when she does this. 'I don't want Freya to hate me,' she says.

'It will get sorted out.'

'Do you think I should go and speak to her?'

'Maybe not right now, Freya's worried about her brother.'

She tosses her long hair.

'Freya might not be ready to speak to you tonight. You might need to give her some time to calm down.'

Ophelia pouts and then she flounces off, not wanting to hear what I have to say. Teenagers.

Sighing deeply, I square my shoulders and concentrate on the next steps. I can't let Ophelia's moods distract me. It's been long enough that I think the police should be called. It's been almost an hour and that's too long for a child to be out of sight. Yes, the odds are that Fergus is still in the building, but every minute is important when a child has gone missing.

I fish my mobile phone out of my bag. It's a heavy old device and my family regularly teases me for having such an ancient piece of technology but I'm not interested in all the apps and extras you can get. I always say I only need a phone to call in emergencies, and now my theory has been put to the test because this is very much an emergency.

Pressing the power button, I will the phone to fire up quickly. The screen slowly loads and it seems to be taking much longer than usual. Perhaps I should've invested in a more modern device after all. I return to the Winchester Room and immediately sense how tense the atmosphere is. I'm guessing that everyone else is starting to think the same as me – it's time to get the police involved.

My phone screen glows yellow and I tap open the keyboard, ready to type in 999. But before I do, the double doors to the Winchester Room fling open.

And there he is – Fergus. In the doorway, appearing wide-eyed but here and unharmed. I cry out with relief, shoving the phone back in my bag, as I race towards him.

'Fergus! Where have you been?'

Other heads in the room turn and I can feel the collective sigh as others clock the missing boy. I drop down to my knees and gather my grandson in my arms. 'Are you OK?'

Fergus doesn't say anything, but I can feel his little body tensing. It's only then I take in the fact that there's someone next to him – a man.

Rocking back on my heels, I get up and clutch Fergus' little hand in mine. I stare at the figure in the doorway, who's wearing casual clothing and sporting a full beard. The man pulls off the black silk mask he's been wearing. I don't recognise this person at first... until I look a little harder.

'No!' I gasp.

'It's me... Aren't you going to thank me for finding Fergus?'

'Jesse!' I pull Fergus closer to me. He's different with a beard but it's definitely him – it's Sasha's ex-husband.

'Don't act so surprised, Nadia,' he says to me. 'I'm sure you guessed that I'd show up here today?'

A shiver slides down my spine. He's right. I came to Burcott House this afternoon because today is Jesse's release date from prison. He was sent down for ten years for manslaughter but he's been let out a little bit early for good behaviour. It seems no criminals serve their full sentences these days. Not many people know that – not even Sasha – but I made it my business to keep tabs on my ex-son-in-law. I had a feeling that he'd make a beeline for Burcott House as soon as he was freed from behind bars. I had planned to come here and warn him to stay away from my family. I was prepared to do whatever it took to get him to stay away. I'd even saved up a hefty sum to try and bribe him to leave us all alone.

When I made my way up the gravel driveway to Burcott House earlier on, I tried to tell myself I was being irrational. Then when I walked into the surprise party, I thought it might be some kind of trap, or a set-up by Jesse. As the evening wore on, I lulled myself into a false sense of security. I was hoping that my gut instinct was totally wrong and that tonight really was a celebration.

I should've listened to my fears. I should've known that it was too much of a coincidence with today being the day of Jesse's release back into the world. I'm sure he's about to cause chaos. And now he's standing here before me, I'm convinced he is behind this surprise gathering as well as being responsible for my grandson's brief disappearance.

This party is well and truly over. But what will happen next?

Chapter Eighteen
Jesse

'Mother-in-law, aren't you pleased to see me?' I tease. 'Because you knew that I was being released from prison today.'

Nadia blanches and she clutches the small boy even tighter to her side.

'Jesse, why have you come back here?'

I stroke my chin, pretending to look thoughtful. 'A trip down memory lane... or maybe I needed to come back to the last place I was a free man before I could move on.'

'You can't be here, surely there are conditions of your release that mean—'

'I've been locked up for years, you silly woman, do you really think I care?' There's a harshness to my words that makes Nadia take a step backwards.

A hush descends in the room around us. There's only a handful of people currently in this big space, many others have either left or are searching for the missing boy, but the guests are cottoning on that Fergus has been found and his return is getting a little complicated.

'Did you take him? Did you take my grandson?'

I bark out a laugh. 'I've just returned him, haven't I?'

Nadia freezes in disbelief. And then something happens that I'm not expecting.

'Daddy!'

She's much taller, but there's no mistaking her – it's my Freya. She sprints towards me, straight into my arms, and I swing her round in a circle, just like I used to when she was little. A lump rises in my throat; all this lost time with her still breaks my heart. Freya always was a daddy's girl and, thankfully, that hasn't changed. I was worried she'd shun me, as it's been a while since she's written or visited. But I saw the way her face lit up; she's missed me just as much as I've missed her.

'Freya, come away from him!' Nadia shrieks behind us.

I peer over my daughter's shoulder and notice how much older Nadia Bailey appears to be now. Almost ten years have passed and I know I have more lines and grey hair than I wish to admit, but there's been a significant change in my ex-mother-in-law. I can't quite put my finger on it, but it's like the big presence she used to have has somehow diminished. She looks more stooped and less in control. Of course, it might be because I've had the misfortune of spending my last decade with some of the country's most hardened criminals that this woman, who I blame for many of the things that have gone wrong in my life, no longer looks intimidating.

Pulling back, I take in my daughter. She's so grown-up. I've missed such an important time in her life. She was almost ten when I was arrested for murder, and it broke my heart to be torn apart from her. Nothing can change the fact that I haven't been present in her teenage years but I'm going to make sure that all that changes now I'm a free man.

'What are you doing here?' Freya breathes in disbelief.

'I've served my time – it's over.'

Freya hugs me again, but much tighter. I've spent ages worrying about whether or not she would accept me back into her life, but there was no need to be concerned. My daughter has forgiven me. She's seen me suffer and she's seen my remorse. I regret what I did. My charge was for manslaughter – the sentence reduced from murder because of the amount of alcohol I'd consumed and because I'd pleaded guilty to hitting Aaron, but not guilty to the intent to murder. I've behaved myself and done everything possible to make sure I got a minimal sentence.

'Get away from her!' Nadia yells, although I notice she doesn't attempt to step anywhere near me. She's still clutching her grandson. This behaviour is definitely different to that of the Nadia of old.

Freya whirls around to face her grandmother. 'He's my dad,' she says calmly, standing firmly beside me and slipping her hand into mine. 'And he's finished his prison sentence now.'

A small cluster of people are staring with open mouths at the scene unfolding. They're not even trying to conceal their interest or their disdain. It feels strange to be out in the world again, let alone back here. But I have a plan and I must carry it out – tonight.

'Freya, this man just stole your little brother. You can't trust him.' Nadia's words are dripping with venom.

Freya's hand slides from mine. 'What?' She gapes at me in confusion. 'Is that true?'

I shake my head. 'Of course not. I found the lad wandering around outside and brought him in, that's all.'

Freya squints at me, and then at her younger brother, and back to me. Suspicion is written all over her face. Nadia may appear different, but she's still prepared to play dirty.

'I didn't even realise he was your brother,' I say to Freya gently. 'How was I to know?'

Freya has told me about her half-brother Fergus but she's never shown me a photo of him. I thought this would help to reassure my daughter, but it increases her hesitation as she studies my face, trying to decipher the truth.

'Is Fergus here? Is he?' A woman with long, dark hair breathlessly enters the room. I haven't seen her for years but there's no mistaking who she is: Sasha. She catches sight of her son and sweeps him up into her arms. Tears cascade down her face as she cries openly.

'Fergus, I thought I'd lost you.'

A man then rushes into the room towards the mother and son. He envelops them both in a big bear hug. The man is tall and broad, and it's obvious to me that this must be Sasha's husband Douglas. It's such an odd thing to see the woman I was once married to being comforted by the stranger who has taken my place. My eyes water and I have no idea why. Sasha and I had fallen out of marital bliss long before the Christmas party that changed everything. I don't know where this pang of nostalgia is coming from – but I guess seeing her with her new partner was always going to be weird.

The little boy is wailing now too, clearly bewildered by all the emotion in the room. Then Sasha's eyes lock with mine. I don't look away; I meet her gaze and I wait for her to break it.

'Jesse?' she whispers, barely audible. 'Jesse, is that really you?'

Nadia doesn't give me a chance to speak, instead she immediately launches into her accusation that I was responsible for Fergus's disappearance.

Holding my hands up in front of me I state again clearly, 'The boy was outside, I guided him back in. That was all. I didn't even know who he was.'

'What are you even doing here?' Sasha's voice is louder, but I can hear the tremble in it.

Before I'm able to explain, Douglas is upon me. He's taller than me and he makes the most of his advantage, grabbing me by my shirt and roughly pushing me up against the wall. 'If you touched a hair on my son's head!'

Gasping, I try to reply, but the pressure on my sternum is too great.

'Dad!' Freya cries, and, as one, both Douglas and I swivel our heads towards her. 'Stop!'

Douglas releases me but I'm more bruised about the fact Freya addressed Douglas as 'Dad.'

'Just get out of here.' Douglas's broad Scottish accent echoes around me but I won't give him the satisfaction of realising that he's got me rattled.

I clear my throat. 'I've spent too much of my life rotting behind bars to mess around. There's something I need to tell you all.'

'You can let my lawyer know. Now get out, before I phone the police.' Douglas draws himself up to his full height and his words are firm.

I look back at Sasha and speak directly to her. 'You're going to want to hear this.'

Chapter Nineteen

Sasha

Jesse is here. In this room. Back at Burcott House. The last hour has felt like a nightmare, not knowing where Fergus was, and the bad dream is getting even more hellish. I'm stunned to see my ex-husband here, I thought he had another few months of his sentence to serve. I thought I had more time to prepare for this inevitable encounter.

'Go on then, what do you need to tell me?'

Jesse has a beard and looks as though he's been spending a lot of time in the prison gym. He worked as a personal trainer when we were married and I'm sure he's taken full advantage of the services on offer at His Majesty's pleasure. I've seen him a handful of times in the last decade, but only when absolutely necessary. We've continued to discuss our daughter's education and I used to accompany Freya on her prison visits when she was younger, but in the last few years she's been going to see Jesse by herself. I should've just cut all contact; maybe other people would say I've made the wrong decision to allow Jesse any involvement in our daughter's life after what he did. But I know it would've destroyed her even more if she hadn't been able to see him at all. She's always been a daddy's girl.

'It's complicated...' Jesse says. 'Can we go somewhere more private?'

Douglas laughs unkindly. 'What a joker. You can think again. Come on, out you go.' He begins to manhandle Jesse towards the door. Despite all the muscles he's built in the gym, Jesse is smaller built than Douglas. I don't want my husband to get involved in a physical altercation with Jesse but I can see he's determined to get rid of the man who has caused me so much pain.

'I swear, it's important,' Jesse states clearly.

'What could you possibly have to say that any of us would want to hear?'

Douglas' words are mocking, but when I look at Jesse's face, I have a sudden bolt of realisation. I think I know what my ex-husband wants to talk to us about.

'It's about Erin.'

I feel as though the wind has been taken out of me. Does Jesse know something about what happened to Erin? Does he know the truth? He can't possibly have worked out what went on the day she went missing, can he?

Goosebumps prickle my skin. My mother and I exchange a look of understanding. We have to hear what Jesse has to say, and we need to get this party closed down immediately.

Before we can communicate further, Leah comes marching into the room. 'They're all going!' she exclaims. 'The food trucks, the entertainers, all of it.'

'That's one less thing to sort out then,' Nadia says. 'Because this party is finished.'

'Is it Fergus, oh God, please—' Leah clocks Fergus in my arms and audibly breathes a sigh of utter relief at the sight of him. 'Fergus is safe, so why are you all looking like it's someone's funeral? What did I miss?'

It's been a frantic evening and there's still a number of people in the room. Jesse blends into the crowd and his beard almost makes him unrecognisable anyway. Leah hasn't realised who he is.

'That would be my fault,' Jesse says, stepping forward.

Leah gapes as she clocks my ex-husband. The pair of them used to be the best of friends. Jesse was very involved in the lives of my family – too involved where Erin was concerned, it turned out – but he and Leah had a genuine, platonic friendship. They were like brother and sister. They're both into fitness and I can remember them running various different marathons together. It took a while for Leah to come to terms with the fact Jesse was a liar, a cheat and a murderer. They haven't spoken since he went to prison.

Leah is stunned and visibly struggling for a way to reply to Jesse.

My mother cuts in and takes control of the situation. 'Let's wind up the party,' she says. 'And then we can all talk properly.'

With that, she goes to the DJ and asks him to announce the party has ended. She then enlists the help of Hayley and Andrew to round up the guests and say goodbye to them. Several people have witnessed Fergus and me being reunited as well as Jesse's unexpected return so it's inevitable the rumour mill about the Bailey family is going to start up once again.

I can't face saying goodbye to the remaining people. There's no way I can fix a smile on and act like everything is OK. And I certainly have no patience for answering intrusive questions, however well-meaning. I indicate to Douglas that we should get out of the main room while the guests are being herded out. He scoops Fergus up in his arms and plants a big kiss on his cheek before steering me towards the snug.

'Freya, come with us,' Douglas says gently to her.

Freya follows us but I'm aware that Jesse is next to her. My skin feels tight and I want to escape my own body, get out of this place and as far away as I can from him. But I must be a grown-up and deal with this situation, for the sake of my children. The last thing I want to do is go over old hurts with my ex-husband and I'm terrified to hear what he has to say about Erin.

When I enter the snug, I see the fire in the woodburner is down to its last embers. The room is still in chaos from when everyone was searching for my son. I'm exhausted, but I've got to keep going and get through this conversation. Then I'm going to leave Burcott House and nothing will persuade me to ever step through the door of this country mansion ever again. Too many bad things have happened here, and I wish that we'd never come tonight.

Taking a seat on a low sofa, I pull Fergus onto my lap. The solid weight of my little boy is comforting and I wrap my arms around his middle. He leans his head back on my chest and sighs. I shouldn't really have him in the room while we're speaking with Jesse but I can't bear to let him out of my sight after the panic-inducing hour when he was unaccounted for. I also need to get to the bottom of where Fergus was during that time and whether anyone was with him.

'Darling,' I whisper into his ear, 'are you OK?'

He nods his head.

'Can you tell Mummy what happened? Where were you? We were all worried about you.'

He shifts on my lap and digs an elbow into my stomach. I wince.

'I was with that man,' Fergus says in a small voice.

'The man with the beard?'

He nods.

'Were you with him the whole time?' I want to try and establish if Jesse really did find my son outside or if he deliberately took him or prevented him from coming back to us.

Fergus is quiet.

'Tell me,' I begin to say. And then I hear his soft and slow breathing. Fergus has crashed out. He's gone to sleep as soon as he curled up on my lap. He's always had a brilliant ability to fall asleep anywhere, any place so I'm not surprised, but I am frustrated that I don't have any information from him about what happened.

Douglas and Freya seat themselves next to me. The space on the sofa is a bit squashed but I'm glad we're all together, on the same side. It means Jesse has to face all of us while he's talking.

It doesn't take long before Leah and Nadia are also in the room. Leah closes the door firmly shut and lets us know that the last of the guests have gone. All my senses are tingling and on alert. I stare at Jesse, waiting to hear what he has to say.

He rubs his throat – I can see red marks from where Douglas pinned him against the wall – and I note Jesse flexing his fingers in the way he always used to do when he was nervous. It's funny how years can go past without spending any time with someone and then when you see them again all their mannerisms and quirks feel familiar once more.

'Jesse, don't keep us in suspense. Why are you here?' my mum asks him.

'I need to tell you the truth,' Jesse responds.

His sentence hangs in the air. Deep in my bones, I know that his next words have the power to change everything.

Chapter Twenty

Ophelia

The scene in front of me all seems very cosy – my family are gathered together in the comfortable snug; they could easily be having a post party drink or a casual end of evening catch up. But appearances can be deceptive and the instant I step into the room I can feel the tension crackling. I've entered at an uncomfortable point and I can tell my arrival has just interrupted something important.

And then I see why everyone is on edge.

I clench my jaw. There's no mistaking the man in front of me. I've studied his photographs for too long. He's dressed casually and has a bushy beard that doesn't suit him at all but I know it's him. The man who killed my dad.

'What is he doing here?'

'Ophelia, there's no need for you to be here. Let's—'

My grandmother is trying to steer me back towards the door but I'm having none of it. I want to know why Jesse Bailey is at Burcott House. I'm sick and tired of being lied to by my family. They can't keep hiding things from me forever.

'I want to know the truth,' I insist.

'We said no more secrets.' Leah takes my hand and then guides me to the armchair next to hers but I don't sit down.

I'm grateful that Leah is on my side and that she's made this part easier for me, because there's no way I'm leaving this room. I turn my attention back towards Jesse. I've spent so much time hating this man, and now here he is in the flesh in front of me. Freya has tried to convince me that her father isn't a bad person and that his actions the night my dad died were completely out of character. It doesn't matter whether what he did was a freak accident or not because the result was still the same. I still lost my dad. Freya and I have agreed not to talk about the past because we just end up getting into an argument. I can't stand to hear her talking about her father, when he's the reason I don't have mine.

I glare at Jesse. His eyes are an unusual shade of amber and he gives me the creeps.

'I said, what are you doing here?' I bark my question out sharply. I can feel the rest of the room collectively inhale.

Nadia starts towards me once more.

'No,' Leah says, waving Nadia back to her seat. 'Ophelia needs to get this off her chest.'

'Ophelia, I've finished my prison sentence. I've come back here because it's time to move on—'

In the past I've been curious about whether Freya had been telling me the truth and if her dad really was just an ordinary person who got caught up in a heat-of-the-moment situation. I knew that if I ever saw him again, then I'd be able to tell. And here he is. And now I know.

He's not in the least bit sorry about what happened to my dad. He hasn't even attempted to make out like he is. Whatever he is here for is all his own agenda and there's no way I'm putting up with it.

'Get out of my house,' I say through gritted teeth.

'What?' Jesse appears to be confused.

'You heard me,' I say a little louder. 'You're not welcome here. Go, before I call the police.'

He holds his hands up in front of him. 'I understand why you're upset.'

'No, you don't. You couldn't possibly ever understand what it was like to find out my dad had been murdered by *you*.'

I stand up and take a step towards him but Jesse doesn't move.

'I've got something important to tell you – to tell all of you.' He looks around the room dramatically.

'There is absolutely nothing you have to say that I want to hear,' I say to him.

'Are you sure?' Jesse challenges me.

I hesitate, the desire to find out more about parents and what happened to them is strong but I also don't want this man anywhere near me.

'I've got something for you, Ophelia. It's a gift.' He stares at me intently.

'What?' I almost laugh. I wasn't expecting him to say that. 'Well, you can take it with you because I want nothing to do with you.'

Jesse reaches into the black bag on his shoulder and then holds out a small, silver parcel in front of him.

'I said no,' I repeat firmly.

'If you want to find out the truth about your mother, then open this box.' He shoves the present into my hands and steps back.

My mouth hangs open. Jesse has just said the one thing that means I will carry on talking to him. Of course I want to open the silver box that's now in my hands.

'Jesse,' Leah says in a warning tone. 'You'd better not be playing games.'

Chewing my lip, I inspect the box more closely. It's a small silver square with a glittery bow on the top. It looks like any of the other eighteenth birthday gifts I've been given but I know in my heart that whatever is in here isn't going to be a simple present.

Glancing back up at Jesse, I notice the way his attention is fixed on me. My stomach somersaults, part of me wanting to hand it back to him. But I must find out what's inside.

My fingers are shaking as I untie the bow. Maybe whatever this contains will lead me to the truth that I've desperately been wanting. Inside is another smaller silver box. I sit down and place the smaller box on my knee.

'What's all this about, Jesse?' Nadia questions. But Jesse remains tight-lipped and everyone in the room is focused on what I'm doing.

Opening the lid of the smaller box, I find a silk pouch. Undoing the drawstring, I slip my hand inside and my fingers hit something cool and smooth. I remove a silver charm bracelet and hold it up to my face. Turning it, I can see a collection of different trinkets attached to the bracelet: a heart, a rainbow, a teddy bear.

Why has Jesse given me this? What does it mean?

Nadia makes a strangled sound and her hand flies to her mouth. Frowning, I glance down at the box and see a handwritten note curled underneath the silk pouch. I read it.

'Is this some kind of sick joke?' I manage to say, placing the item of jewellery down on the low coffee table in front of me.

Nadia paces over to me. 'I know who that bracelet belongs to.' She rips the note from my hand and I watch as the blood drains from her face.

She reads the note aloud: 'Missing you, always.'

A figure steps out of the shadows at the back of the room and I almost scream in shock.

And then I see who it is.

It's my mum. It's Erin Bailey-Scott.

Chapter Twenty-One

Erin

I try not to smile at the stunned faces in front of me. The room has gone so quiet you could hear a pin drop. I remain still, waiting for someone else to make the first move. I've thought about this encounter for a long time. Countless nights have been spent awake, tossing and turning, imagining the different ways in which I could reappear in the lives of my family. Nothing could be more fitting than to resurface at Burcott House.

I poured so much of myself into shaping this hotel into a successful business, but it was more than that to me: it was my passion, my home – and it should've paved my way to freedom. I was planning to use the money from the hotel business to build a new life for myself. But that was before this gorgeous property became the location of my downfall. Now I'm hoping to rise again like a phoenix from the ashes.

Everything hangs on tonight. I've been building up to this, turning potential outcomes over and over in my head. I can't afford to fail.

I decided it would be more impactful if I remain silent when my mother and sisters first see me. And I was right about that. Saying nothing stretches out the uncertainty and the magnitude of my return. It also allows each and every member of my family to come to terms with the fact I'm still alive. I watch as their expressions change from disbelief, to acceptance, to panic. Because the truth is, however much they may have pretended otherwise, most of the people in this room prayed I was dead.

Unfortunately for them, I'm very much alive.

Someone screeches, a loud and unbearable sound that almost makes me cover my ears but I remain poised and unruffled. A young woman who is not my daughter but looks pretty much identical to her is the source of the noise. This must be eighteen-year-old Freya. She's certainly changed from the freckle-faced child I remember her as, but so has everyone here. Time has marched on while I've been away.

My mother seems older than I remember her, but still fierce and proud. Sasha has changed the most – her clothes, the way she does her make-up, and her posture all suggest a woman who's a lot more confident and self-possessed than the version of my elder sister that I last crossed paths with. My younger sister Leah is exactly the same except her hairstyle is shorter. It suits her. She also has a certain glow about her that makes me think she's living well.

The high-pitched screech is still slicing through the air and my thoughts. A large man I've never met before leaps into action to calm Freya down and his soothing Scottish lilt works almost instantaneously, the girl's hysterics quickly toning down to a whimper.

'Is... is she a ghost?' Freya manages to whisper.

I almost laugh out loud at that. I'm not of course, but perhaps if I had died on the mountain that day I would've come back in another form and haunted the women who abandoned me to the elements. Thankfully, luck and resourcefulness meant I survived that terrible ordeal. But in the months afterwards I was plunged into a horrible nightmare as I recovered and tried to figure out what to do next.

Leah is the first to speak. 'Erin, is it really you?'

She rises from where she's sitting and moves so she's inches from me. I take her in, my little sister; she is one of the most innocent people in this room. So many others have secrets they're hiding. Leah doesn't deserve to be caught up in this, I have no cause to hate her. She catches my hands in hers and smiles faintly.

'It really is you!' She grips my fingers between hers. I wasn't expecting an emotional reaction from Leah – or myself. Not after all my plotting and planning. I swallow and push down the feelings swirling inside me. This isn't the time to get sentimental.

I nod in response. 'I'm back.' I keep it simple, not wanting to give too much away at this stage.

My eyesight snags on the scar on the left side of her face. She used to cover it up expertly with layers of make-up but she's favouring a more natural look these days. An old feeling of guilt suddenly washes over me. Leah got that scar because of me – I was out of control and driving a car. I didn't mean to do it, Leah stepped out into the road. It was a freak incident, a case of wrong time and wrong place.

No-one believed me, both Sasha and my mother turned against me. I'd always been the outsider in the family and the accident cemented my position. I often wonder where we might all be if that car accident hadn't happened. Although there's no point on dwelling on what ifs... it happened and I'm sure Sasha and my mother would've found another way to express their true feelings about me if it hadn't.

This idea snaps me back into the present. I've waited for this day for what feels like forever and I need to make sure that I don't waste this opportunity.

'I can't believe it,' Leah is half laughing and half crying.

I need to keep control of the situation. Looking around the room my eyes alight on the flame-haired girl I've been longing to see. I step around Leah without replying.

'Ophelia...' I open my arms wide. My daughter pauses and it's obvious she's unsure how to react. It's been so long since I tucked her into bed at night – those minutes just before sleep when she'd rattle off the highlights and lowlights of her day are the moments that I missed the most.

Finally, she steps into my embrace. I draw her tightly into me and breathe in her sweet-scented hair. I don't want to let go of her. She's my darling child, my baby girl. I've hated every day we've been apart. I think back to when I used to gather her to me like this when she was little. Ophelia was always the affectionate one whereas her twin, Jasper, was less open with his feelings. I loved them both equally – and I've never stopped loving my babies in all the time I've been away.

'Mum,' she whispers into my shoulder. 'You're here.'

I reluctantly pull back then, kissing her on the forehead before drinking her in. She's grown so much since the days when I was the mother who raised her – I used to comb her hair in the morning, collect her every afternoon at the school gates and read her stories each evening. Now, she's a woman herself and I barely know her. She's tall and willowy, just as I thought she would be, and she's the spitting image of me at the same age. It's easy to see the resemblance between the two of us. We have the same heart-shaped face, the same colour eyes, even the same shade of hair. There's no doubt whose daughter she is.

The whole room is in hushed silence, watching mother and daughter reunite. I cast my eye over the people in the cosy snug room –

one of my favourite spots in the building – and I'm surprised to see Sasha wiping away tears. I have no idea why she's crying and, more importantly, I don't really care. My heart hardened towards my sister a long time ago.

I push down my emotions. It's time to get things started.

'My mother and sister haven't been completely honest with you, Ophelia,' I say, loud enough for everyone in the room to hear.

Ophelia's face clouds with confusion. 'What do you mean?'

I turn my head away from my daughter but I don't hesitate to answer, I plough onwards. 'They're not who you think they are...'

Ophelia goes to speak again but Nadia's voice booms, 'Erin, think about whatever it is you're about to say. You've destroyed this family twice already... don't do it again.'

Nothing she says is surprising. 'I was expecting you to say that, of course. It's not like your daughter has just returned from the dead or anything! I thought you would've at least spared me ten minutes before you began your usual tirade against me.'

'Erin, *please*. We've all missed you. We have. Let's not go back to where we were. What about a clean slate, for all of us? Let's start again?'

She walks towards me, a strained smile on her face. But if my mother thinks it's going to be that easy then she's completely deluded.

I crook my eyebrow. 'Do you really think that's possible?' I make sure my voice is lower, reeling her into a false sense of security.

'Yes, I do,' she says more softly. 'Whatever has happened, you're still my daughter.'

Nadia is standing in front of me. Ophelia is looking anxious and Sasha puts an arm around her. The sight makes my anger flare. Sasha is comforting my daughter, just as she's done for years, while I've been out in the cold.

I laugh. 'There's no way the slate can be wiped clean, not after everything that's happened.'

Nadia stares at me, trying to assess what my next move is.

'I missed out on my children. I've had a half-life, and it's time that things changed.' I say all this as clearly as I can. I'm finding it hard to keep a grip on my raw emotions. Blinking rapidly, I try to keep the tears at bay.

And then Jesse is next to me, linking his hand through mine. I smile up at him, his presence strangely reassuring. He gives me a small nod, and I know that's our signal to lay out why we're here.

I turn to the rest of my family: Nadia with her arms folded and a dark expression on her face; Sasha with one arm around my Ophelia and one arm around Freya; the man who I assume is Sasha's latest partner gripping his small son tightly on his knee.

'We want our children back.'

My demand rings out clearly and I watch as it lands with every single member of the Bailey family.

'And we aren't leaving until that happens,' Jesse follows up. I recognise how emotional he must be feeling.

Sasha hugs Ophelia and Freya to her more tightly. 'Stay away from them!'

Her shrill voice rings in my ears. But nothing and no-one is going to stop me now...

Chapter Twenty-Two

Sasha

'Erin, you can't come marching back in here demanding for things to change. Where have you even been?' I shout at her. Shock waves are flooding my body. I can't believe Erin is here in this room. Alive.

I know I should try to remain calm and collected but that's difficult when faced with my ex-husband and my missing sister. And even more difficult when they're threatening to take away Freya and Ophelia. Both girls are pressed against my sides. I'm not letting them go, because I don't trust Erin and I certainly don't trust Jesse with their care. If they believe they can just swoop in and take these two away, then they are very much mistaken. They've got the fight of their lives on their hands.

'How? How did you survive?'

Here she is, right before my eyes. She looks exactly the same. Still as glamorous as ever, her green eyes meet mine in a way that makes my heart skip a beat. Erin has always known what she wanted – and never stopped until she got it. I was a fool to think that my sister had perished.

Of all the things that could've gone wrong at this party today, this was not something that crossed my mind. I have so many questions that it's hard to put them all into order. I'm completely baffled by

Erin's return. For many years, I tried to convince myself that she had died – it was the only way I could try to move on with my life. Except deep down, in the very core of my being, I just knew that my sister hadn't perished. For years, I was constantly looking over my shoulder, expecting her to come crashing back into our lives. But it didn't happen. Until now.

As time went on, the intense media interest in Erin's disappearance simmered down. It never completely faded away, it was always there in the background, but it was less all-consuming. It was the same with my emotions – a few years after her disappearance I managed to stop obsessing about my missing sister. It was hard but I had to do it in order to move on. Douglas and I married. Then when Fergus came along it was like a new phase in my life. I immersed myself in the baby bubble and, when I eventually returned to work, I felt like a different person. Fergus's birth marked the end of the worst time in my life. Since then, I've tried to push all thoughts of Erin from my mind. With each month that went by, the fear of her coming back gradually ebbed away.

My guard was well and truly down – I hadn't expected her to stay away for this long without returning. Erin is many things but she was a devoted mother and I can't fathom how she kept away from the twins if she was living and breathing in another corner of the world.

'Why have you stayed silent all this time?'

Erin crooks an eyebrow at me. 'You mean, why didn't I respond to any of the media appeals?'

Raking my hands through my long hair, I feel exasperated already. 'Why didn't you just come back?'

'Has it occurred to you that I may have been seriously hurt? That I might have suffered memory loss or physical injuries?'

Given her French-manicured fingers, her well-put-together outfit and her sleek hair and make-up, it hadn't occurred to me. Erin looks just as flawless as she did before the ski trip that changed everything. There are no signs of trauma or long-lasting damage to her body. She seems unscathed and as perfectly presented as she ever did.

Erin shrugs her shoulders. 'I went through a lot.'

'Really? And yet this tough life of yours has involved expensive shopping trips and manicures?'

'Sasha, don't try to be smart. You know nothing about what's happened to me.'

'That's right. So tell me.'

Erin has pink splodges on her neck, a tell-tale sign that she's infuriated.

'It took me a long time to recover from falling from that mountainside.'

'But it was almost a decade ago,' I press on. 'What has stopped you from letting us know that you survived? We all thought you were dead.'

She stays tight-lipped. My body is filled with nervous energy and I'm determined to get some answers. For Ophelia's sake as well as mine.

'Why have you stayed away?' I ask again. 'Do you not realise we've all been going out of our minds wondering what happened to you?'

'Oh please, don't give me that. Spare me the act, you don't need to keep pretending.'

Her words chill me. How much of the truth will spill out of her mouth tonight?

'Why won't you tell us where you've been?' The questions are flowing from me, unfiltered. I want to know why she's stayed away and why she's chosen to come back to torment us. Knowing Erin, there's more to all of this than she's letting on. If I can just figure out what game she's playing, then it'll help me to protect the girls.

'I'm sure it hasn't made any difference to you,' she says. 'It's not as though we were close before the skiing trip.'

'Not made any difference?' Erin's words kick my fury up a notch. 'I've helped to raise the children that you've ignored! Do you not understand how much they've missed you? How much they needed you? Why did you not come back for them?'

Her face is pinched and a vein is pulsating at her temple.

I turn away. Freya is shaking like a leaf and silent tears are rolling down Ophelia's cheeks. She's so vulnerable. I recall the countless evenings when I've held my niece in my arms and let her cry out all her frustrations. Seeing Ophelia's distress makes me whirl around to face Erin once more.

'Aren't you going to answer? Can't you at least be honest about this? Or are you going to carry on being selfish?'

I'm pushing things too far. I should stop but I can't help myself. Ophelia and Jasper are my family, I've loved and looked after them like they're my own children in my sister's absence. Despite everything, we've done OK. I've got them both to the point where they're starting to thrive. I can't bear for Erin to catapult back into their lives and to ruin it all.

'Selfish?' Her tone is no longer measured. 'You have no idea what it's been like! You have no idea how much my heart has been breaking without the twins. Being with them again is all I've wanted.' Erin pauses then and sweeps her eyes around the room.

'Where's Jasper?' she asks, directing her question at Jesse. 'Is he joining us soon?'

'Jasper isn't here, thank goodness,' I shoot back at her, thinking it's strange that she has only just noticed his absence. This kicks my suspicion up a gear because if she was really back for the sake of the twins then Jasper as well as Ophelia would be the focus of her attention.

'What do you mean, he isn't here?'

'He's in America,' I say, and then immediately regret sharing this information with her.

Erin gasps. 'What is he doing in America?'

I decide not to say any more and keep my mouth shut. The last thing I want is for Erin to go flying out to Jasper and start disrupting his life. As far as I'm concerned, she lost the right to do that when she decided not to return to her twins sooner.

'He's studying out there,' Ophelia murmurs, before I can cut her off.

'What!' Erin thunders. She rounds on Jesse. 'You said that everyone would be here tonight?'

'I thought they would be,' Jesse trips over his words.

'My son not being here is a pretty big oversight!' Erin's tone is ice-cold. The united front that the two of them portrayed just a short time ago is falling apart already.

My mind is in overdrive. Erin and Jesse have been keeping in touch. But Jesse has been in prison and Erin couldn't have gone to visit him, given her missing person status, unless she was disguised? Or have they been communicating in another way? One question leads straight on to another.

'Why do you want to be back in the twins' lives now? Just be honest, for once in your life. Don't you think your daughter deserves that?'

'I don't have to tell you anything,' Erin growls back at me. 'I will say this though, coming back here has been the hardest thing I've ever done. Even harder than being stranded in sub-degree temperatures in the snow. And you know why.'

I swallow, fearful of what she might say next.

She points her finger at me. 'If you want to talk about the truth, then let's talk about the truth.'

'Erin,' Nadia interjects with a warning note. 'Think carefully about what you're saying.'

'Oh, I have thought carefully about it. I've had a very long time to think about things.' Erin's eyes glitter as she looks at me. 'Sister, you're right. Let's play our game of truths.'

Chapter Twenty-Three

Erin

'What you really want to know is how I survived the fall from the mountain, is that right?' I say bluntly.

Sasha steps closer to me, her hand stretches out but then she lets it fall by her side and stops. She's shaking her head.

'Is that what you meant? Because you saw me go over the edge of the mountain, didn't you?'

'Erin, please don't do this,' my sister bites back at me. Her tone tells me that she's still the same old Sasha and the years I've been missing have clearly done nothing to soften her heart where I'm concerned.

'Or did you mean, how did I survive the kick you gave me that sent me spiralling?'

'Erin, stop!' Sasha shouts, trying to drown out what I'm saying, but she's unsuccessful. My accusation is ringing around the high-ceilinged room.

'Sasha?' The man comforting Freya, the person I'm guessing is Sasha's new husband, sets his little boy next to him on the sofa and springs to his feet. Several deep frown lines etched across his forehead.

'Oh? I don't believe we've met,' I say sweetly to him. 'I'm Sasha's missing sister. The woman she tried to kill.'

I deliver the words precisely and it feels good. I've been waiting almost a decade to make this revelation.

His face falls. It seems my dear sister Sasha has not told her handsome beau what really went on the day I was lost in the snowstorm.

'Sasha, is this true?' Douglas's eyebrows have gone so high, I swear they're about to disappear into his hairline.

'Douglas, she's twisting things. Just like she always does. Don't listen to a word she says – she's poison!'

Sasha is already distraught. And so she should be, because she nearly did finish me off. I don't feel one ounce of sympathy for her, not after what I've been through. Besides, this is just the beginning, I've got plenty more in store for my elder sibling tonight.

Douglas is comically torn between believing the woman he loves and the new information that he's just been given about her.

'Is this true?' he asks again incredulously.

Fluttering my eyelashes coyly I say, 'Something tells me that you know the answer to that question.'

Douglas groans deeply and sinks back down into his seat. If everyone looked shocked when I appeared in the room it's nothing to their reactions now. I'm enjoying this.

'Douglas, no – she's only just got here and she's causing chaos. Don't let her worm her way into your head...' Sasha rambles on, trying her utmost to convince Douglas that I'm crazy.

Catching Jesse's eye, I give him a small nod. He's been my lifeline in so many ways, even if things aren't exactly running to plan. I can't believe he didn't work out that Jasper wasn't going to be here. Although there's nothing that can be done about it.

'Erin, what's the meaning of all of this?' Nadia circles me, obviously trying to figure out my next move.

'What? No hug? No welcome home?' My words are loaded with sarcasm; I knew my mother would be the last person who would want me to rise from the dead. I'm sure she's been relieved to have me out of the picture for all this time. It's not like we've ever really got along and she's never tried to properly connect with me. I've caused her far too much family drama and I'm a little too headstrong and complicated for her liking.

'I... I don't understand?' For the first time I can remember, Nadia looks like she doesn't have things under control.

'You don't understand how I managed to claw my way back to the land of the living? Why's that, Mother? Perhaps it's because you witnessed me crashing down that mountainside as well?'

Douglas's head jerks up sharply. 'What? You were in on this too?'

Now I do laugh, long and hard. Flashbacks crowd my mind of Nadia's televised appeals and radio interviews in the months after I went missing, pleading for information about me and wringing her hands for my safe return. I was impressed at how well my mother acted out her pretend grief and reeled in the media with her lies. She could've won an Oscar with her performance.

'Seriously? You were both there, on the mountain?' Douglas' head swivels wildly between his wife and his mother-in-law, disbelief written across his face.

'The Bailey family always have secrets,' I chuckle. 'Haven't you figured that out by now, Douglas?'

'Erin, don't do this. You know exactly what went on and you've got no-one but yourself to blame.' Nadia narrows her eyes as she's talking to me.

'That's not how I remember it,' I say slowly. 'The way I see it is that you chose to help Sasha over me. And then as you were pulling Sasha to safety, she gave me a nice big kick on her way up. She knew exactly what she was doing. She wanted rid of me.'

'Mum – tell me that didn't happen?' It's Freya who's gobsmacked now. She's utterly stunned by the idea that her prim, proper, rule-abiding mother could do anything wrong.

Sasha hangs her head, not saying anything. Her silence shows her guilt. Douglas scoops up a bleary-eyed Fergus, who has half-woken up because of all the shouting.

Douglas puts the sleepy boy over his shoulder and announces, 'I'm taking Fergus and Freya home.'

I'm surprised; I didn't expect that Douglas would bail on his wife so easily. From what I'd heard, the pair of them are completely besotted with each other. Although I suppose the news that your wife tried to kill her sister could change your opinion of someone pretty fast.

'Douglas, wait!' Sasha's chin is held high. 'You have every right to doubt me. You have every right to be disgusted with me. You have every right to walk away but, before you do, just think about what you know about me. Then think about why I might have done that.'

Sasha's eyes are ablaze and she continues on, 'Because it's true. I did kick Erin – I kicked her as hard as I possibly could because she deserved it.'

Everyone in the room is holding their breath, including me.

'I wanted her dead.'

'You wanted your sister dead?' Douglas repeats, bewildered. He shifts his weight from one foot to the other and moves Fergus onto his other shoulder.

'Yes, I did. Because it was her life or mine.'

Chapter Twenty-Four

Erin

Then

My breath is coming out in icy puffs in front of me. I cling with one hand to the slippery mountainside while the other grips to my sister Sasha's cold hand.

I'm terrified. I'm one wrong move away from death, suspended in mid-air over an unforgiving drop of thousands of feet. I've just made the biggest mistake of my life. I got too close to the edge.

You'd think the second attempt at murder would be easier. But perhaps after how easily my husband Aaron went over the bannister at Burcott House, I've got too cocky. And this is where it's landed me.

My mother's face looms down over the ridge of the snowy ledge above us. I'm not sure if I'm hallucinating. How can she be here? But when she starts to talk, it becomes clear that she is really there and this is my chance to survive this ordeal. I blurt out my apologies, saying anything to try and save my own skin.

Nadia reaches down to Sasha first, just as I knew she would. There's no way she would've gone for my hand first. I tighten my grasp around

Sasha's hand but I can feel her own grip going slack. That's when I know. Just before she does it, I guess what she's going to do.

Sasha's going to do what I would've done. Pull away with her hand and kick out with her foot. Her snow boot connects with my head, but my guesswork has given me a fraction of a second to bring the hand that was in Sasha's back to the mountainside. I cling on hard with both hands. My feet are precariously placed on the ledge beneath me but, thankfully, Sasha's kick wasn't very forceful. I remain where I am, in the same dangerous position as before.

I don't want my mother and sister to know this. Sasha has kicked me, with the intention of killing me off. And my mother has made it clear whose side she's on. I can't trust either of them to reach down and pull me to safety. I scream, loudly and convincingly, the way I imagine someone would if they were freefalling to their death.

Holding my breath, I expect one of their faces to come back into sight, peering down to check if I really am hurtling to the ground. I wait, but it doesn't happen. Their voices move away, becoming more distant with every heartbeat.

That's when I panic. Have I made the wrong decision? Am I just going to be stuck here forever? Will I be found frozen in the snow days or decades from now?

I almost scream for my mother and sister to come back but I know it's too risky – I have no idea if they'd help me or hurt me. I gingerly press down on the ledge I'm balancing on. It's sturdy enough, for now. I inch sideways slightly, gently testing each step to the right with my foot before putting my full weight on it. I can see the ledge curves upwards and I might just be able to get to the point where I can crawl back over the side.

Those minutes are the longest of my life, using my feet to feel along the mountain ridge. My teeth chatter and several times I almost lose my balance. I don't look down; I keep focusing on each baby step until I reach a wider section of the ledge. Assessing it, I realise there's a section that widens and then another sheer drop. I've come to an impasse; this is as far as I can go.

I am higher and it could be possible for me to haul myself up over the side of the mountain, to safety. I close my eyes briefly and gather my courage. As I do, I become aware that my fingers are feeling stiffer than I'd like. My whole body is freezing up. I've got to do this otherwise I might really become an ice statue.

It's now or never. Live or die.

I don't know how I manage it, but I get myself up over the edge. Then I immediately surge forward, as fast as my body permits, through the deep snow. My skis are out here somewhere; I navigate as best as I can in their direction. Luck is on my side and I find them. Hurriedly, I strap them to my feet. If Sasha or Nadia had taken the skis or hidden them, then getting back to safety would've been more difficult. I briefly worry I'm going to make obvious, followable tracks but the snow is falling so hard I doubt that will be an issue.

Before I push off, I pull my phone out of my ski jacket. Well, a phone, my burner phone. I ring one of the two numbers on there. It connects: there's signal, more luck is on my side.

'I need you to do something for me,' I say rapidly.

The cooperation of the other person at the end of the line is vital because I already know I can't go back to my family. I've no doubt Sasha will go to the police to let them know my part in Aaron's death if I try and return to the ski chalet. There's only one thing for it. I try not to think of Ophelia or Jasper. If I do then I might falter in my course of action.

The only way for me to survive is to disappear.

Chapter Twenty-Five

Ophelia

Now

'STOP! Can everyone just stop!'

I can't take this anymore. I wanted to find out the truth about my family's past, but now I wish I could rewind the clock back a few hours and wipe my mind clean of the information I've discovered. I never once thought that my aunt Sasha, of all people, was responsible for my mum's disappearance. Or that my grandmother was involved in it too. It's all just so screwed up.

'None of this makes sense! Jasper and I were told that you were alone when you went missing, that no-one had seen you. If... if you were both there then, that means everything has been a lie.' I throw my arms down to my sides but I don't say anything else. I can't trust myself to speak anymore, my emotions are overwhelming.

Sasha shifts uncomfortably from one foot to the other. 'I'm sorry Ophelia, it didn't quite happen like that. But I can give you an explanation, if you'll just listen?'

I give a small nod in response. Out of the corner of my eye, I notice that Douglas sits back down on the sofa. He needs to hear this too.

'I kicked Erin because she pushed me over the mountainside first, she tried to kill me. I knew she would always be after me, so it really was me or her.' Sasha points in Erin's direction, her eyes accusing.

'I saw it all happen,' my grandmother Nadia adds. 'I witnessed everything. Erin shoved Sasha but the two of them went over the side of the mountain. I believed I'd lost them both. It was only because of the ridge just below the edge that they didn't both die.'

Douglas makes a strangled noise. He sounds how I feel. This is a lot to take in.

'But how could you leave my mum there? In those freezing conditions?' I'm speaking as if I'm in a dream-like state, none of this feels real.

'Exactly—' My mum tries to take charge of the conversation again but my grandmother is having none of it.

'I thought she'd lost her grip and fallen to the bottom,' my grandmother says loudly. 'I'd also just seen her try to kill Sasha. What Erin isn't telling you is why we were on that mountain edge in the first place. Erin had chased Sasha to the brink and pushed her over. She was trying to kill her. I had to think about the risk to Sasha's life too.'

'And there's more,' Sasha adds, pausing and looking at me directly. 'I'm sorry Ophelia, I never wanted you to find this out. Except now I see it's important for you to understand what happened.'

I suddenly feel cold in this thin, pink dress even though the evening is fairly warm. My eyes dart between the two women who've been there for me in my teenage years, the women who stepped into my mother's shoes. I believed they were there to help me. I thought they loved me. But have they just been lying to me all along? And how can I trust what they're about to say next?

'Your mother killed your father,' Sasha tells me. Her eyes bore into mine as she's speaking. The truth hangs in the air between us.

'What did you just say?' I don't think I can have heard Sasha properly.

'Your mother was the reason your father died,' Sasha repeats. 'The whole thing was a set-up. She organised everything and she stood behind Jesse as he ended Aaron's life. That's the secret about your parents that we've been keeping from you.'

'Don't listen to her, Ophelia,' my mother Erin demands.

Blood rushes to my head and I block out everything else that's going on in the room. The only thing I can focus on is my mum's face. The face I've pored over in so many photographs since I last saw her.

'Noooooooo...' The sound escapes my lips as I'm still processing the latest lie that's unravelling.

'I'm sorry, love,' my grandmother says. 'Your father died because Erin and Jesse wanted to be together, and they also wanted your father's money.'

The walls feel like they're closing in.

'What?'

A red mist descends over me. Like the kind I used to get when I was a child. I hear someone roaring, yelling. And then I realise it's me. I rage, in a way that I haven't done in years, repeating the same word.

'No! No! No!'

'Ophelia, Ophelia?' Freya's familiar face swims in my blurry vision. My cousin is by my side. Her cool hands on my clammy arms bringing me out of my fit of emotion.

'It will all be OK,' Freya says gently.

I shake my head because I very much doubt that. Sasha's words hammer in my mind but can I believe what she's telling me? The truth feels so twisted.

I reach for Freya and put my arms around her neck. She holds me close to her. 'I'm sorry,' I whisper to her. 'About Levi.'

Freya grimaces a little but says, 'Don't worry about it.'

'Ophelia, sweetie, let me help you.' My mum stretches her arms out towards me but I flinch away from her.

'Don't come near me!' I shriek.

My mum's face blanches. 'Ophelia, honestly, you're not going to believe all the things they're saying, are you?'

My mouth gapes. I don't know what to believe but as soon as Sasha uttered the words 'Your mother killed your father', it made sense. The missing piece of the jigsaw puzzle. In the last few months, I've been on a quest to find out more about my family's past. My mum's poisonous rant made me suspicious about my grandmother and my aunts. When really, she was the snake all along.

I take in my mum: her glossy hair, her designer clothes and the expensive smell of her perfume. She doesn't come across as someone who's been struggling. She looks the exact opposite. Then I remember the way she and Jesse stood together when she first entered the room. They were shoulder to shoulder. I feel sick. I can't process this.

This isn't how I imagined this reunion. I've been longing for this day ever since my mum went missing. I would have done anything, absolutely anything, to have her back – alive and well. Here she is, only inches from me, but I don't want her near me. The sight of her is making my skin crawl.

'You didn't tell me that you and Jesse were an item,' I say, a sharp edge to my words.

'I didn't think it mattered.'

I'm shocked by her response. It feels like the ground is shifting beneath me as I realise that I really don't know my own mum at all. If this is her response to her relationship with Jesse then could it be true that she was involved in my dad's murder? I can't even ask that question, it's too big.

'Didn't think it mattered?' I leap towards her, just inches separating us. 'That man killed my dad – your husband!'

My mum bites her lip, in exactly the same way I do. Having her here makes my heart ache and burn at the same time.

'Why didn't you tell me that you were in touch with Jesse?'

'There hasn't been time...'

'Hasn't been time? Oh, but there has, hasn't there?' I pull myself up to my full height. 'Because as we're sharing secrets, I'd better tell everyone mine.'

I gaze around the room at the rest of my family. They aren't going to like what I'm about to say.

'This isn't the first time I've seen my mum since she went missing.'

'You mean, you knew she was alive?' Sasha's face is filled with disbelief. 'How long have you known?'

'Yes, but only recently. Earlier on this year, on the anniversary of the day she disappeared, she called me.'

My mum smirks and anger spikes through me once again. I trusted her but if she was involved in my dad's death, how can I forgive her? Especially when she has Jesse by her side. I didn't know that she had involved him in the plans for this evening. And I had no idea they were plotting a future together.

'How could you keep that from us?' my grandmother asks. She moves to the window and stands with her back to all of us. Her shoulders are tense, her body held rigid.

'I... I... I don't know.'

My heart sinks. I didn't think I was making a mistake. I was overjoyed that my mother was alive and that I had a second chance with her. I couldn't believe it; it was like a dream come true. To be with her – living, breathing, smiling, laughing – was everything I had wanted since the day she disappeared.

She told me not to tell anyone, not even Jasper. It's been a real struggle to not say anything; the weight of the secret has been pressing down on me. But she said she wanted to get to know me first and then return to the family on her terms. After a month or so of long phone calls and snatched, too-short meetings, she told me that she wanted to organise an eighteenth birthday party for me and Jasper, a night to remember, and that she would attend.

I was delighted. I'd badly wanted a big party for my milestone birthday anyway and my mum said it would be her way of trying to make up for all the birthdays she had missed. I couldn't persuade Jasper to come home but I didn't tell my mum that because she had been very clear that all the family needed to be at the celebration. I was working so hard to cover up the fact my twin wouldn't be here that I didn't question her wanting to re-enter our lives in this way. I was just thrilled to have her back. I've been naive. I didn't ask enough questions on why she hadn't returned before or where she'd been. When I tried to get her to tell me about how she'd survived and what really happened to her, she said she would tell me everything but I just had to be patient. I was happy to go along with her ideas because I just wanted my mother back.

I helped her to organise the invites and it was my responsibility to make sure everyone came. I made up an excuse to meet my grandmother here earlier today – that was easy. Coming up with an invite list to the kind of celebration I've wanted for years was even easier. I made sure to include my grandmother's friends, extended family for both the Baileys and the Scotts, as well as plenty of my friends. When Freya got her invite, I encouraged her to pass the date on to loads of her mates. She was the only person who knew I was aware the surprise party was happening. Although she had no idea I was involved in sending the invites out.

Although, I didn't completely lie to my grandfather when I said I hadn't organised everything. Because the only part I sorted out was the invites. It wasn't me who pulled everything else together. That was my mum. She kept asking me what kind of thing I'd like at the celebration and she nailed the food trucks and masquerade ball. It was a shame the DJ wasn't better but she did a decent job considering she organised most of it from afar.

I've been looking forward to this party for months but it's not what I thought it would be. There are things about my family that I didn't know about – didn't understand.

I wipe a hot tear from my cheek. I feel so hurt. Why has my own mother lied to me?

'Did you really plan my dad's murder with Jesse?' I finally pluck up the courage to ask.

She hesitates for too long.

My view of the world flips in an instant. I've put my mum on a pedestal. I believed she was a good person, a loving mother, a devoted wife who lost her husband and then was involved in a tragic accident. I got it all wrong.

'Murderer!'

The word cuts through the silence, slicing like a knife and severing the connection between me and my mum.

I pick up the charm bracelet my mum tried to give me and I fling it at her.

I can't take back my words. And she can't change her past.

As far as I'm concerned, I no longer have a mother. She is dead to me.

Chapter Twenty-Six

Nadia

I stare out of the window, looking up to the full moon hanging in the sky, listening to Ophelia and Erin's revelations. I feel tired, bone tired. I don't have the energy to deal with all of this and yet I know I must. It is time for all of our family secrets to come out, once and for all, and it's time to deal with them.

Sasha is shouting at Erin, telling her exactly what she thinks of her return. I close my eyes and wonder how we all got here. And what will happen next.

Although I knew, in my heart, this day would come. There had to be a resolution to what happened to Erin. The search for her was high-profile, it featured in the news in the UK and Europe every day for months. She was a beautiful, wealthy socialite whose husband had just been murdered. The police and local mountaineering volunteers carried out an intensive search for her for over three weeks. When her body wasn't found I always suspected it was because she got away.

Energy was also poured into trying to find Craig Turner, my first love and Sasha and Erin's father. He'd already been in prison for decades for murder. But he'd been released and turned up at the ski resort the day Erin went missing. His arrival also coincided with the untimely death of Xavier Knight, who was a friend of Erin's. The young man's body was discovered in his ski chalet and there was a lot of speculation as to whether there was a connection between Erin's disappearance and Xavier's end. Craig was the prime suspect for both and when the police found him, they arrested and charged him for killing Xavier. They questioned Craig extensively about Erin's whereabouts but he maintained he didn't know.

After a few weeks, the authorities dialled the search back. Hugo Scott, devastated by the murder of his only son and then further saddened by the disappearance of the daughter-in-law funded a private search operation that continued for several more weeks. I was numb with guilt. The idea that my daughter might've died and I hadn't saved her weighed heavily on my heart, while at the same time I was fearful that she would return and try to hurt Sasha again.

We've all lived in limbo ever since, so at least everything is coming out into the open. Despite it always having been a possibility, I'm stunned that Erin survived. The conditions on the mountain that day were treacherous and I heard her falling with my own ears, didn't I?

My mind has started playing tricks on me as I've got older. Thinking back over my life, I question what was a lie and what was reality. There have been many twists and turns in the relationships between my three daughters. I've tried to be fair; I've tried to help all three of them. But now it's time to do what is right, for the future of our family.

I turn around. 'Enough.'

My mouth is set in a grim line. I know what I need to do.

'Erin, it's time. Are you going to tell everyone the truth?'

Erin places her hands on her hips and crooks an eyebrow at me. 'I don't know what you're talking about.'

I sigh. 'Let's end the games. Tell them what you did.'

She shakes her head, the light catching in her glossy, red-brown locks. 'Stop trying to drag up the past. It's done with now; we all need to move on.'

'If you won't confess your crime Erin, then I will.'

Erin rolls her eyes at me, like she used to do when she was a teenager.

'It's true. Erin was involved in Aaron's death,' I say clearly. 'I saw it happen.'

Ophelia's jaw drops at this.

'Erin was right behind Jesse, telling him what to do. She was urging him on; I can remember her words. She said: "If you want me as much as you say then prove it. Now." Jesse pushed Aaron over the bannister that night, but Erin was the one who planned it.'

Ophelia wobbles unsteadily, as though she's been dealt a body blow. And then she starts to crumple.

'She's going to faint!' Douglas warns.

'Catch her!' I say, springing towards my granddaughter but knowing that I won't get to her in time.

Sasha does the same but neither of us manage to break Ophelia's fall. She tumbles to the floor and there's a sickening crack as her head hits the corner of a glass coffee table.

'Ophelia!' I exclaim.

It's Erin who gets to her first. Ophelia is out cold on the floor, a small trickle of blood oozing from her temple.

Erin gathers Ophelia into her arms but there's no response.

'Ophelia, Ophelia...' Erin murmurs, caressing her daughter's face.

'Don't move her too much,' Sasha instructs, going into teacher mode.

'We need to call an ambulance – and the police!' Leah sounds hysterical.

'No!' Erin says. 'No police.'

'Ophelia's hurt, we can't just...' Leah garbles, pulling her phone from her pocket.

'I said no!' Erin screams back at her, dislodging Ophelia from her lap and flying towards Leah.

Leah puts her hands out to ward Erin off, but it doesn't do anything to deter her. Erin snatches the phone away from Leah and puts it in her own pocket.

'We're not involving the police,' Erin repeats.

'Do you seriously care more about your own skin than looking after your daughter?' Leah asks. The question hangs in the air and I'm sure we all come to the same conclusion. Erin has already proven that she's cared more about saving herself than coming back for the twins.

I kneel down next to Ophelia; Sasha is on the other side of my granddaughter. I can see that she's checking Ophelia over thoroughly.

'She's breathing,' Sasha tells me.

I exhale. For one horrible minute I thought the fall might've been fatal. 'Her pulse?'

'Still steady,' Sasha replies. She leans over and kisses Ophelia on the cheek. Then, like a sleeping beauty, Ophelia's eyes flutter open.

'Are you OK, love?' I ask, full of concern.

'My head...' Ophelia groans. 'What happened?'

'You fainted,' I remind her, hoping she's just a bit foggy rather than there being anything significantly wrong with her memory. Her head connected with the edge of the table with some force.

'See, there's nothing wrong with her,' Erin declares. Her green eyes are flashing with an emotion that I can't quite put my finger on.

Ophelia catches sight of her mother and it's clear that tonight's conversation comes flooding right back to her. My chest loosens: her memory is thankfully fine. I'm just sorry my granddaughter has such difficult information to grapple with. She starts to shake her head in distress.

'Ssshh,' Sasha soothes. 'Lie still, you had quite a knock.' Sasha cradles Ophelia in her arms, and the colour gradually begins to return to my granddaughter's face.

Satisfied that Ophelia isn't too seriously hurt, I rise to my feet and turn my attention back to Erin.

'Come on Erin, it's time for you to tell us. Why are you really here?' Instinctively, I fold my arms, bracing myself for more lies.

'I told you. Jesse and I want our children back.'

Speaking slowly, I say, 'They're hardly children anymore. You've missed them growing up. So why are you returning now?'

'I was always planning to come back for them, it just took me a little longer than expected.' Erin is looking down, avoiding my scrutiny. I've lived enough to know that not making eye contact when speaking is a classic sign of someone lying.

'If you won't tell us then I'm going to fill in the gaps. You fall off a cliff in sub-zero temperatures, manage to get yourself to safety. Even accounting for some months of discovery, you must've at some point clocked the huge media circus that was going on around your disappearance. How did you manage not to be seen? Where were you living? I'm guessing someone helped you, am I right?'

Erin smiles tightly. 'Very good.'

'Was it Jesse? Helping you with contacts outside of prison?' I'm going to keep chipping away until we get to the truth.

'You're just dying to know, aren't you?' Erin teases, glancing at Jesse in a way that suggests he's in on the secret.

My blood boils. Erin has always had the power to rub me up the wrong way, she's very similar to her father. I fight to keep my composure; this is important and losing my cool isn't going to help. But I'm not going to stop – as a family we all need to know the truth to make sense of the past and to work out where we go from here.

'Your children are already grown, there must be another reason you're here.'

'You should've been a detective, Mother dearest,' Erin says, trying her best to wind me up.

'We want a relationship with our children,' Jesse interrupts. 'We've both missed out on too much.'

He sounds choked up in a way that makes me think he's genuinely missed Freya and that's why he's returned to Burcott House. But something tells me I'm right to think Erin's motive for showing up tonight is very different. There's more to her return.

I try to think rationally. It was Jesse's release day, so it's clear that Erin organised the party tonight to coincide with that. At least I've found out who was responsible for arranging the surprise birthday celebration. My hunch earlier was correct. I wish I had just stopped the evening in its tracks instead of allowing the event to go ahead, then perhaps we might not have played straight into Erin's plans.

But why did she wait for Jesse to be released to come back? He's been in prison, surely he could only help her so much. And, knowing my daughter, she didn't need his support to reveal to us all that she was still alive.

There's something niggling me about who helped her in the aftermath of the accident on the mountain. Alarm bells are ringing. I'm hoping that I'm going down the wrong track, but I should really start listening to my instincts. My overwhelming feeling as I look at my middle daughter is to get myself and the rest of my family as far away from Erin as possible.

Erin can't be trusted.

She'll stop at nothing to get what she wants.

But I won't let her destroy my family again.

Chapter Twenty-Seven

Sasha

The past is unravelling tonight. Part of me is relieved the truth is coming out but the other part of me is scared about what else might be revealed – and who might get hurt because of it.

Ophelia has just had some painkillers and seems to be recovering after her fall. She gave me a fright but I can't dwell on this too much as Jesse is talking and I need to concentrate on his words. I just hope he doesn't have too many more surprises in store.

'I just want to spend some time with Freya, for us to get to know each other again.' Jesse appears to be nervous as he says this. He's watching Freya and waiting for her reaction.

'I want that too, Dad,' Freya replies instantly. 'I'm glad you're here.'

My precious daughter hugs her father. When she pulls back from the embrace, I hear Freya whispering to him, 'You took all the blame for Aaron. Why didn't you tell the police Erin was the one who planned the whole thing?'

'It's complicated.' Jesse's answer is short, suggesting he doesn't want to delve too much into this with his daughter in front of everyone else. He looks pained. Protecting Erin and not sharing the part she played in Aaron's death has resulted in him spending years behind bars, missing out on his daughter growing up.

'I missed you,' Freya says quietly. My heart contracts, I know she missed her father but hearing her say this now, her voice full of sadness, makes me wish things could have been different.

'Come with me then,' Jesse says to Freya. His words are smooth and there's an inviting smile on his face. 'We could go on holiday somewhere – anywhere you want. Paris? Vegas? New York? I've saved up to take you on the trip of a lifetime.'

'Hang on,' I interrupt the father–daughter exchange, panic beginning to course through me. I never wanted to cut Jesse out of our lives but I didn't expect him to catapult himself so suddenly back into our midst. I thought I would at least have been given some warning so I could prepare myself and plan how to go about handling his contact with Freya. 'Don't you have conditions you need to meet with the prison? And are they aware you're planning to leave the country?'

Jesse spins round; he's been caught off guard. 'I can sort all of that.'

I hate how this must sound to Freya. Her father has just offered to make her dreams come true and I'm jumping in to take the opportunity away from her. But Jesse should never have said all that to our daughter without discussing it with me first. He didn't even let me know his release date, and the thought of his deception makes my stomach do somersaults. I let myself believe that after so much time spent behind bars, he would leave a reformed man. I thought his betrayal was a one-off and I assumed he would respect the fact that I allowed Freya to keep in touch with him.

I've continued to allow the contact between Jesse and Freya because Jesse has communicated so well when it came to anything to do with Freya – both before he went to prison and during his sentence. I was prepared to navigate the conversations with him for Freya's sake. I didn't want her growing up not knowing who her father was, when he still cared for her deeply. I grew up without knowing much about my own father and I didn't want that for my daughter.

This is the first time I've had any doubts about Jesse's behaviour where Freya is concerned. He's never mentioned a fund for taking Freya on a trip before. I'm not comfortable with this idea at all. Especially not this soon. And especially as Jesse has showed up here with Erin.

I take in the two of them. Jesse keeps glancing towards Erin, like he's hoping for her to support his cause. But she's looking away, out the window. It's as if she's caught in a momentary daydream and I wish I knew what she's thinking about. If only I could read my sister's mind, so much heartache could've been avoided.

And then Erin does look at Jesse. A small smile plays across her lips but I can't tell what it means. I can't tell if they're returning just as friends with the same aim of seeing their children or if there's something more to their relationship. Maybe they never cooled their love affair.

I feel sick. I believed I was Jesse's only lifeline to the outside world. At first, I hated it but over time I made peace with the situation. I couldn't change the past but I convinced myself that Jesse wasn't a bad person and that he'd just been caught up in a temporary madness. He certainly acted as though he was full of remorse. I held onto the idea of the person I thought Jesse was when we first met. I did what I could to support him because I thought that if Jesse and I could model a healthy relationship, and Freya knew that she was loved by both of us, then it would make the fallout of Jesse's actions less painful. I wanted her to see there were consequences to every action but I also wanted to teach her that love and forgiveness were important values too.

If Jesse has been in contact with Erin the whole time he's been in prison, without telling us, then that means he's been lying to us every single day. And he's effectively thrown all the patience and kindness I've shown him back in my face. There's no way I'm allowing Jesse anywhere near Freya on his own, I need to get to the bottom of what's been going on between him and Erin.

My attention has been on Freya and my ex-husband during their exchange. But that's not the only problem I have to contend with. Douglas is sitting on the sofa with his head in his hands. Miraculously, little Fergus is somehow still sleeping, laid out on the sofa beside Douglas. I'm sure he's exhausted after the party and everything that's happened since.

I breathe deeply. I need to take charge of this situation and I know what I have to do next.

I give Douglas a look, the one I always give him that's a secret signal between the two of us when we want to leave somewhere. And I certainly want to get out of here.

'Well, nice as it's been to see you both,' I say, as though Erin and Jesse have just popped in for a normal social call. 'It's getting far too late and I have a very tired child that I need to get to bed.'

Looping my arm through Freya's, I guide her away from Jesse. 'It's time we were leaving.'

Douglas is staring at me, his eyes red-rimmed. I'm willing him to play along, willing him to come with me so that we can escape this madness and go home with Freya and Fergus. All I want is to be in the safety of our cosy house and to be curled up on the sofa together, his reassuring arms around me. After tonight's revelations, I don't know if that will ever happen again. I'm scared that he will refuse to even talk to me, let alone that the pair of us can go home together like nothing has changed.

To my relief, Douglas shifts in his seat. I can tell that he wants to be out of here too. A glimmer of hope makes me think he will listen to my side of the story; he will give me a chance. I've got to convince him that everything I did was to protect myself and Freya. I just pray I can make him understand.

Because I can't lose Douglas, he's the love of my life.

Before Douglas can prise himself off the sofa, Erin begins laughing. 'Leave? You want to leave now?'

'I do. It's best we all get a good night's sleep and talk again in the morning.' Douglas is firm in his delivery.

Erin's laughter echoes around the room once more. It disturbs Fergus and he begins to toss and turn in his sleep. My attention snags towards my son before flitting back to my sister. The chilling expression on her face startles me. It's a look I've seen once before – on a cold mountainside just before she tried to kill me.

'No-one is leaving here tonight.' Her voice is like ice.

'Don't be ridiculous, Erin,' I shoot back at her. 'You can't trap us all here.'

'Really?' Erin smiles back at me. 'Go ahead then. Try to leave.'

I feel as though someone has thrown a bucket of freezing water over me. So this is what she was up to. I can't believe she's lured us to Burcott House with the intention of backing us into a corner. Why would she do that?

I stride towards the internal door at one end of the room and try to yank it open. It's jammed shut and it doesn't budge, however hard I try. Erin wasn't bluffing. I go across the room to the only other door but I get the same result. My breath catches in my throat but there's still one more escape route that she may not anticipated. Rushing towards the big bay window, I grab the window handle and push forward. I was expecting the glass panel to fly open but it doesn't. I shove it one more time but to no avail. Erin has even made sure the windows are sealed.

Whirling around, I see her watching me through narrowed eyes. She doesn't make a move or a sound. A silence settles in the room as everyone takes in what Erin has done and what it might mean.

'I don't like this,' Freya says meekly.

'Neither do I,' Douglas adds, moving Fergus's legs from his lap and standing up. 'I don't know what game you're playing but that's enough. Let us out.'

Erin puts her hand on her chin and looks thoughtful. 'Well, seeing as you asked so nicely... No.'

Douglas gapes at Erin. He's only just beginning to process how dangerous my sister is. 'Just unlock the door,' he tries again.

Erin pouts and doesn't respond.

'Douglas and the kids have nothing to do with any of this. Can you just let them go?' I hate the pleading note in my voice but if I can just get a few of my loved ones out of the room that would be something. And it might provide an opportunity for the rest of us to escape as well.

'What? So he can go and alert the police? I don't think so.' Erin isn't going to be a pushover.

'I don't need to leave to do that,' Douglas says, pulling his phone out of his pocket and hastily unlocking the screen. He manages to type in '99' before the mobile is knocked from his hand.

'Not a chance,' Jesse grunts as he bends to retrieve the mobile device he's just shoved to the floor.

In the split-second Jesse's head is down and vulnerable, Douglas pounces. He takes an elbow to Jesse's exposed back and forces him to the floor. My eyes bulge in surprise. I wasn't expecting Douglas to react in that way as he's usually calm and level-headed.

'What the...?' Jesse starts to say but the wind is knocked out of him and he sprawls face down.

Douglas throws his full weight on top of him, pinning him to the highly polished wooden boards. Seconds later, Jesse is thrashing under him. Douglas is much taller and heavier so I hope this means he has the advantage over my ex.

I'm momentarily frozen but Erin is filled with rage. 'Get him off you!' she's screaming at Jesse. It seems she didn't factor my new husband in her plans tonight.

'Douglas!' I spring into action, grappling with Jesse's legs and trying to still them. Except Jesse is kicking with everything he's got and I can't get a firm hold. I'm so focused on my task that I don't see what Erin is doing. I just hear the sickening crash followed by a painful groan.

Flicking my gaze upwards, Erin is holding a brass trophy aloft. Previously, it was sitting on the mantelpiece but now she's brandishing it like it's a weapon. And Douglas is laid out on the floor.

'What have you done?' I yell at her.

I just manage to rock backwards and avoid a sharp kick from Jesse as he rolls away from me. There's no point in trying to leap after him and my concern is only for my darling Douglas. I'm instantly by his side and I cradle his head in my arms.

At my touch, Douglas lets out a whimper of pain and his eyes open wide.

'Oh,' I manage, a sob rising up in me. 'Are you OK?'

'Silly question.' Douglas smiles faintly back at me. I have no idea how he can tease me at a time like this.

Swiping his hair back from his forehead, I check him over but I can't see any major cause for concern.

'I moved as she came at me,' Douglas explains. 'She missed my head and clobbered me in my back instead.'

Dropping a kiss on his forehead, relief courses through me that he hasn't been seriously harmed. But if we all stay locked in this room it's only a matter of time before someone gets badly hurt – or worse.

'I want all of your phones,' Erin barks, flinging Douglas's mobile device on the coffee table.

No-one moves. 'Now,' she demands.

'Why do you want our phones?' Ophelia questions. Her face is tight with worry – and Freya is wearing the same anxious expression.

While Ophelia is distracting Erin, I discreetly extract my phone from my clutch bag. If I can just get through to the emergency services then someone will be able to come and help us.

I manage to unlock the phone but it's snatched out of my hands before I can do anything else. Erin hurls it onto the table and I watch the screen shatter as it hits the smooth surface. Douglas catches my eye and I can tell he is as worried as I am.

I observe as Jesse takes Freya's phone, more gently, but he's still taken it. He's acting like some kind of henchman to Erin – I still can't work out what the current dynamic is between the two of them.

Without our phones, and with all the doors and windows locked, our odds of getting out of this room are very slim. There are only three possibilities left. The first is to try and break the windows, but I happen to know they're triple glazed and therefore will be very tough to make a dent in. The second is to try and convince Jesse or Erin to let us out, which doesn't seem likely at this point. The third is to get the door key because one of them must have it. I think option three is our best chance of escaping.

I have to get my family away from my deranged sister as fast as I can. Because I'm afraid that if we stay locked in this room together for too long, then one of us will die here.

Chapter Twenty-Eight

Jesse

'What's going on, Daddy?'

Freya's green eyes are sparkling with unshed tears. I squeeze her hand in mine but my response sticks in my throat. I've spent what feels like forever yearning for the day when I'd be reunited with my daughter again so the last thing I want to do is frighten my precious girl. The truth is, I don't know what's going on. This was not part of the plan.

Or it at least it wasn't *my* plan to lock everyone in this room. I had nothing to do with it and I was just as shocked as everyone else when Sasha couldn't get out of the doors or window. I'm sure Erin has got it all figured out but why hasn't she told me? I thought we were in this together. I thought she'd told me everything and that we were partners in this return to Burcott House and the Bailey family. But now I'm not so sure.

'It'll be OK,' I say softly to Freya.

Erin is marching towards Nadia, poised to wrestle the last mobile phone from her mother's fingers. I expect Nadia to resist but she doesn't – she just hands it over without any fuss. Why is Nadia going along with this, has she realised something that I haven't?

My wrist is throbbing from where I fell on the floor, my back is bruised and my head is foggy. Being released from prison and then returning straight here, to the place where my life went so wrong, maybe wasn't such a good idea after all. I should've given myself a bit longer to adjust to the outside world. But I was eager to get to Freya as soon as I could and Erin was eager to put our plans to confront the Bailey family in motion.

I believed I was strong enough, both mentally and physically, to handle whatever was thrown at me once I was released from prison. Because I've had time on my hands to think everything through and to get myself into the best physical shape I've ever been in. I thought I was ready for this but being on the outside again is more overwhelming than I imagined it would be.

The world has moved on while I've been languishing at His Majesty's pleasure. This house has changed. My family has changed. Even mobile phones have changed. How did I think it would be easy to jump back into my old life, or at least a version of it?

'Erin.' I keep my voice low as I get closer to her but she either doesn't hear me or she's ignoring me.

I catch her wrist in my hand, signalling for her attention, but she wrenches her arm away from me like she's just been burnt.

'Erin,' I hiss through clenched teeth. 'Tell me what you're doing.'

This is the first time since we cooked up the idea of returning to Burcott House on my release date that I've questioned what we're really doing here. Erin and I never lost touch. She's kept in contact with me either by writing or phone calls if she could – although they've all been under the guise of another persona because of her status as a person missing, presumed dead.

Fixing her eyes on me, she smiles faintly. 'You still don't get it, do you?'

'Get what, Erin? Tell me. Because all I know is that we both came back to get our children – together.'

Erin laughs, throwing her head back, her expensive earrings glittering in the artificial light. Her behaviour is spooking me.

I'm dimly aware of everyone else in the room going still, tuning in to our exchange.

'Come on Erin, this is what you want too, isn't it – to take the kids and go somewhere, anywhere else but here?'

Erin shakes her head. 'That's what you wanted.'

My jaw goes slack, I have no words to form a response. I'm confused. The tone she's using has an edge to it. She isn't speaking to me the way I'd imagined, given I'm meant to be the love of her love and we've only just been reunited.

I close the gap between us and cup her beautiful face in my hands. I've always thought her green eyes were otherworldly and her delicate features pixie-like. I've dreamt of Erin and I finally getting the chance to be a couple. I could see a life for the two of us – and our children – somewhere hot and sunny. Maybe Brazil or Thailand. Anywhere where we can have a fresh start.

I drop a kiss on her lips. She stays still for a moment; I can almost feel her kissing me back. But then she pulls away, spinning out of my arms. And I can feel the evening and all our plans for the future spinning away with her.

'We said we'd be together.' My voice cracks with emotion.

Erin looks down at the floor.

Memories of the two of us flood my brain. I was dating Sasha when I first met her sister Erin. Erin's energy was infectious; she made me feel like I could do anything. I tried hard not to hurt Sasha but I couldn't stop myself from falling for Erin. Something clicked when we were together in a way that I'd never experienced before.

I'd decided to leave Sasha, be honest with her and come clean. But then she found out she was pregnant with Freya. There was no way I was going to leave her then, I wanted to be part of my child's life. And Nadia made it very clear she'd make my life hell if I didn't support her daughter and grandchild.

I was heartbroken but I told myself it was my punishment for being a cheat. Erin left and became estranged from the family. In some ways that made things easier, in other ways much harder. I committed myself to being a family man, to being the best father and husband I could. Things weren't perfect but I showed up and I stayed. Until Erin came back into my life.

She sought me out and rekindled our flame. I knew then I'd do anything to be with her. But I didn't realise that she'd test me to my limit and make me prove my love for her in the worst possible way.

I killed a man. I killed Aaron Scott. When I close my eyes, I still hear the thud as he hit the marble floor. I swallow down bile. But Aaron was a bully and Erin needed me to protect her from him. I just wish things hadn't gone that far.

I would do anything for Erin. I've proven that by going to prison and waiting until we could be reunited again.

'We said it would be the third time lucky.' I hope my reminder of this will bring her back to her senses. I want her to remember how much I've given up for her and how much I want this to work.

'*You* said it would be third time lucky,' Erin quips back. 'But you've never been very lucky, have you Jesse?'

'What did you say?' My body is starting to tremble. This is the woman I've loved for half my life, the person I've risked everything for. Why is she talking to me like this?

'Jesse, it's always been you leading this "thing"...' Erin makes quotation marks with her fingers and I feel like I've been slapped '... between us. I've just played along with it.'

'You played along with it?' I repeat her words back to her, trying to process what the hell she means.

She's nodding at me. I feel like I'm in a nightmare or I'm tripping because this can't be real.

Erin suddenly sweeps her arm across the table, throwing all the mobiles to the floor. One by one, she stomps on them, crushing the links to the outside world as she does. Her actions snap me out of my panic. She isn't thinking straight, this has all been too much for her. That must be why she's acting like this.

'Calm down!' Sasha demands in her schoolteacher voice. Of course, this doesn't calm Erin down; instead it has the opposite effect. She's in a frenzy destroying the electronic devices.

'Erin, don't. Let's just—'

She jumps away from me when I try to reach out for her. She's slipping through my fingers but I can't let go of my dream just yet. I wait, like I've been waiting most of my adult life, for Erin to stop what she's doing and come back to me. Finally, she pauses and a look of peace washes over her face.

Over Erin's shoulder I see that Ophelia and Freya are huddled in close to Sasha, who has her arms protectively around both of them.

Douglas and Nadia are at one of the doors. They're up to something but I couldn't care less about either of them. Erin is my priority; she always has been.

'Erin,' I say gently. I'm convinced Erin's losing her mind right now. If I remind her of our plans, of the two things that bind us together, then maybe it will snap her out of the emotional rollercoaster she is on.

'Ophelia and Jasper. The twins. *Our* twins. Remember? It's our chance for us to be together, as a proper family.'

Erin's eyes meet mine and I'm sure I've got through to her.

'*My* twins, actually,' she says smoothly. 'They were never yours and never will be. Aaron was their father.'

I frown. 'No, no Erin. You told me they were mine. You told me... Ophelia and Freya, they both look so alike. It must be true!' I'm floundering, my body is trembling with shock. 'I believed you.'

'Well, you shouldn't have.' Her words are so clipped, so cold. The harsh truth is sinking in, ripping through me and turning my insides out.

Years ago, Erin informed me that Ophelia and Jasper were my children. It's why I reignited our affair, why I left my marriage, and helped her get rid of Aaron. She made me think that her bully of a husband was making life difficult, not only for her but for my biological children as well.

'Why would you lie to me?'

'Why would you believe me?'

'This isn't a game, Erin; this is my life. I've rotted away for years in prison. Because you said you needed me to help you, for the sake of our kids. You said you loved me. Why would you put me through all of that?'

'Jesse, you forget that you had a choice in all of this. Just like you had a choice originally between me and Sasha. You chose Sasha. You broke my heart.'

Erin's voice wavers and I think it might be real emotion. But, then again, she's proven herself to be an excellent actress. I should never have trusted her.

I feel sick. Is she trying to tell me that she's punishing me for the decision I made to stick by Sasha when she was pregnant with Freya? I've told her that I regretted it, that I only stayed because I didn't want Freya to grow up without me. And I've told her repeatedly that it's her I love, more than anything.

'I always vowed I'd make you understand heartbreak too one day. And now that day is finally here.'

'What?! You're telling me it was all about revenge? Don't you get that my heart has been breaking every day since I got sent down for the crime that you made me commit!'

I start to feel like the walls of this room are closing in on me. I've spent too many hours in a small cell and I didn't expect to go from one locked room to another. I've never liked being indoors – I've always been an outdoorsy type. So being forced to spend the majority of my days in a cramped cage with another person has been extremely hard.

I want to get out of this room.

Erin Bailey-Scott never loved me. She just used me to get what she wanted. I've wasted the best years of my life loving her. She thinks I'm a fool, and I am.

She must also think that she's so clever, for duping me. I bet she believes she's broken me.

I'll let her think that. But I won't let her get away with what she's done to me...

Chapter Twenty-Nine
Ophelia

Oh my God, what have I done?

I believed that my mum being alive would solve all my problems – but she's not who I thought she was. This woman is nothing like the smiling woman I remember from my childhood. The person who made pancakes on the weekend, conjured up silly stories and was there with arms open wide at the school gates at the end of every day.

More than once this evening I've wondered if this really is my mum, or just an evil imposter. But there's no mistaking the person in front of me – she's definitely Erin Bailey-Scott. It doesn't seem as though she's aged a day since I last saw her, like she's been frozen in time. So why is she acting so differently?

I dig my nails into the palms of my hands. Finding out she was still alive was a dream come true. And when my mum told me that she'd come back for me and that she'd missed me every hour we were apart, I was over the moon. I believed her. I've been daydreaming about what it would be like to go on shopping trips and spa days together. I thought we'd become the best of friends as well as mother and daughter.

But watching the intensity of the argument ping-pong back and forth between her and Jesse makes my whole body tense. He isn't my favourite person in the world but the way she is treating him is horrible. I'm stunned to hear her talking so heartlessly about my dad. I blamed Jesse for my dad's death and I've hated him for it. Now, he has accused my mum of forcing him to kill my dad. And she isn't denying it. She was involved in my dad's murder too...

She's not the mother I knew: she's dangerous and frightening. What have I done bringing her back into our lives? It's been a big, big mistake. I want her to leave and never come back. But she's got us all locked in the snug and she's spiralling out of control.

I don't like it one bit but what can we do?

My head is aching from my tumble earlier and I can't think straight, my mind feels jumbled with worries. Sasha taps me on the arm and pulls me out of my anxious thoughts.

'We need to get the key to the door,' she tells me quietly. 'One of them must have it.'

I nod in agreement.

'Will you help me get it?'

'Of course I will,' I whisper back to her.

I curse myself for giving my mum the skeleton key to the hotel earlier in the evening. She'd asked me to get it for her and I blindly did exactly what she asked me. After I'd searched my mum's study, I snuck upstairs to one of the guest bedrooms where she was hiding out for the evening, ahead of her big return. If I had any idea that she'd then use the key to lock us in here, I would never have given it to her.

Sasha's expression softens and I realise she was worried that I was involved in Erin's plan to lock everyone in this room. She couldn't be more wrong; I'd never do something like this to the people I love.

'I'm sorry,' I say. 'I should've told you that my mum was still alive and that she'd contacted me. I very nearly did... but she said I shouldn't tell anyone.'

Sasha remains quiet, so I go on.

'I didn't think she'd be like this. I just wanted the mother I remembered back.'

'I know,' Sasha says whispers. 'I understand why you did it.'

'Do you hate me for bringing her back?'

'No, not one bit. And how could I hate you, you're my niece.'

'Well... after everything she did to you,' I nod towards Erin. 'And it's because of me that she's here.'

'Ophelia, sweetheart, Erin will do what Erin wants to do. She always has. Don't blame yourself for her actions, she would've found a way with or without you.'

I sniff, trying to stop myself from becoming emotional. 'Everyone says I'm like her...' This worry has consumed me. I'm seeing my mum's true colours. Is this how everyone sees me too? Is this why Sasha reacted like she did when she found out I'd kissed Freya's boyfriend?

'You look like her,' Sasha says gently. 'Although that's where the similarity ends. You've got a good heart, even if sometimes you get things wrong.'

I bite my lip. I know Freya, sitting on the other side of Sasha, is absorbing this conversation too.

'Do you forgive me, Freya?'

Freya looks over at me. 'Yes,' she says simply.

Sasha breathes a sigh of relief. 'I wish things had been that easy between me and Erin. How did we get here?'

She pats my hand. I can't change the things that have gone on already tonight but I can try to do something to get us out of here. I just need to find that key and unlock the door. My focus switches to Jesse and my mum. Jesse looks like he's going to break down. From what we've heard of their heated exchange, my mum has been stringing him along for years and she's chosen now to tell him there's no future for them.

What a bitch.

I can't see that my mum has a bag with her. Jesse had a jacket with him though and it's currently slung over the arm of a chair. The door key could be in one of his pockets. Slowly, I tiptoe over to the denim jacket and dip my hand into one pocket – it's empty. Then I try the other. There's no key but there is a mobile phone. That's something at least. I grab it and duck down behind the chair. Fumbling, I manage to open the emergency call option and I punch in the number for the police. The phone connects and I hear the dialling tone.

Jesse is shouting at my mum but it'll only be moments before they spot what I'm doing.

'Hello, police quickly. I'm trapped—'

'Can you let me know your name, location and a number to call back on if we get disconnected.'

'I'm at Burcott—'

But that's all I can say. My mum whips the phone out of my hand and ends the call. Her face is like thunder.

'WHAT do you think you're doing?'

I glare back at her defiantly. She knows exactly what I was doing.

'You're my daughter, how dare you call the police! You nearly ruined this!'

'I've nearly ruined this? You've ruined everything! You've tried to destroy this family over and over.'

'They deserve it. One day, you'll understand why I've done the things I've done but you need to choose your side wisely.'

Folding my arms, I give her an icy look. 'You pretended that you were dead and you've only just returned because it suited you. You've lied to every single one of us in this room. And you want me to choose a side? Are you for real?'

She is taken aback, as though she never expected me to do anything other than hero-worship her. Given our interactions in the last few months, I can see why.

'I don't choose *you*.' I jab my finger towards her. 'I choose my real family. Every. Single. Time.'

Sasha is in my peripheral vision and I can see her expression of approval and delight as I'm saying this. In contrast, my mother's face is pinched tight.

'Is that how you really feel?' she asks me.

I nod, stepping back to be next to Sasha and Freya. The people who have been there for me when I needed them the most. I link arms with Sasha, making my feelings very clear.

'You'd better be sure, Ophelia,' my mum says, warning me. 'Because there's no going back after this.'

'I am.'

Her face flushes a deep pink. She's angry with me, but I've made my decision. After what I've seen and heard tonight, there's no way I want anything to do with her.

'You'll regret this,' she snaps at me.

'That's enough, Erin,' Sasha steps in.

'Oh, but you see, it isn't.' My mum grimaces. 'I'll decide what enough is.'

Her eyes are wild. She's about to say something else to us but there's a noise on the other side of the room and her attention is drawn to the door.

'Hey, what do you think you're doing?'

My mum races to the door and pulls my grandmother away from it. The two women tussle, each trying to gain the upper hand. Douglas is still fiddling with the lock. My grandmother tries to hold my mum away from him and the door to give him more time to open it. But my mum breaks free and claws at Douglas, breaking his concentration.

Douglas groans and throws his hands in the air. 'Impossible!'

I'm guessing he was trying to pick the lock. Unfortunately, he's not been successful. At least he tried. Douglas is a good guy, one of the best, and I know he'll do whatever it takes to get us out of here.

'It won't work, you're wasting your energy trying to get out of that door,' my mum cackles.

Douglas brushes her off and turns his attention back to the lock.

'I mean it, there's no point.'

'There's always a point. There's always a reason to keep trying.' This is a phrase I've heard Douglas say over and over. I used to think it was annoying; he often rolled these lines out when he was trying to encourage me to do my homework. This is the mantra that Douglas, my generous and patient step-uncle, lives his life by. My heart squeezes. I don't want my mother to hurt the people I love – and who have loved me. Growing up, I've felt like I didn't have a proper family. Tonight has opened up my eyes to who they really are.

'There isn't actually,' My mum gloats. 'Because even if you did get out of this room, the whole hotel is in security lockdown. So you won't be able to leave the building. There's no way out.'

Douglas gives the door an uncharacteristically vicious kick. I open my mouth to say something, but Sasha gets there first.

'Why are you doing this?' Sasha confronts Erin. She looks as though she might slap her, but instead she balls her fists at her sides.

'Because it's time to finish all of this, once and for all.'

'Finish what?' Sasha challenges her. 'We've got this family back on track. We've been doing so well. What makes you think you can come back here and—'

There's a loud bang and it makes me jump so hard I fly forward a few paces. What was it?

Bang. Bang. Bang.

I can't see where the noise is coming from. And then I see it. A face at the window.

I suck in my breath.

'Who's that?' Freya voices my question. It's dark outside and the lighting in here is dim. It's hard to make out who the person outside is.

I can see fists flying, pummelling the glass panel so hard it must hurt.

My grandmother crosses the room and the figure on the other side stops what they're doing.

'Hayley!' Nadia cries. 'Hayley, you've got to help us!' Her voice goes full volume, in her attempt to get her message out as clearly as possible.

My stomach swirls with a mixture of anxiety and excitement. Our cousin Hayley is outside. Someone knows we're here. It feels like we're closer to getting out of this room. I rush over to the window and peer out. I try to see if anyone else is with Hayley but she's alone.

She's slightly muffled and I just hear the word 'Out!'

'What did you say?' Nadia shouts back through the glass.

'You've got to get out!' Hayley's voice is much clearer and there's no mistaking her meaning. Why is she telling us to get out? Does she know that my mum is inside or is something else happening?

Then my mum is at the window too. Hayley reels back in shock. I'm not surprised by Hayley's reaction. Hayley must think she's seeing a ghost.

Shoving me out of the way, my mum grabs the heavy curtain and yanks it closed. Hayley vanishes from view. If the hotel really is in lockdown like my mum says then Hayley can't get in. And if Hayley can't get in, does that mean no-one can? If the emergency services arrived, would they even be able to get to us?

My heart rate speeds up. 'You can't do this!'

'Oh, but I can...' my mum responds. There's a manic air about her.

'You can't just keep us in here forever,' I storm back at her.

'Don't worry. Everyone will be leaving very soon.'

Then she takes something out of her pocket and holds it out in the palm of her hand for me to see.

I'm praying that it might be the door key, but it's not. My brain kicks into gear and I realise what she's showing me.

My heart was pounding before but now it feels like it's going to explode.

'No! Don't do this!' I yell.

Chapter Thirty

Erin

I never intended to involve my daughter in all of this. But she's sided with the rest of them. I've been away for too long and Nadia and sisters have brainwashed her. I expected her loyalty to remain with me because I'm her mother and we had such a close bond. Seeing her with Sasha has pushed me over the edge. I clearly can't trust Ophelia so I've got to change my course of action. I don't want to but there isn't any other way.

I take in Ophelia's beautiful face. It's like looking at a mirror and seeing my past being reflected back at me. She is my double and I remember how I was at her age. I had my whole life before me, just like her. But, as I discovered, life can take a downward turn very quickly.

'Oh Ophelia. Why couldn't you just have chosen me?' I reach for her but she brushes me away.

My mind becomes saturated with memories as I stare at the woman who was once my little girl. I'm stung by her rejection, my heart weighing heavily in my chest.

The next thing I know, Ophelia's hand is closing around my wrist. Is she reaching out for me? Changing her mind?

No, her fingers press too tightly into my flesh and her other hand is trying to prise the little box away from me.

I've let my guard down. I shouldn't have paused and given her this opportunity. If I've learnt anything by now, it's trust no-one. There's an expression of steely determination on my daughter's face. Maybe she is more like me in personality than I gave her credit for.

'Give it to me.' Ophelia is pressing her nails hard into my skin but I'm not going to release my grip, however painful this gets.

'She's got a box of matches!' she yells to the other Bailey women.

I clutch the little box tighter. Ophelia takes a step back and I think maybe she's given up but instead she launches herself at me, scratching at my face.

I wasn't prepared for that. The matchbox tumbles from my grasp as I fight to get her off me. But I don't stop, because we're both dropping to the floor, scrabbling after the matchbox.

Ophelia reaches out first but, as she does, I manage to knock her off balance and she goes sprawling across the floor, letting out a little yelp as she hits the unforgiving wooden floorboards.

The matches are back in my hand once more and there's not a moment to lose.

Nadia and Sasha are distracted as they help pick Ophelia up. I don't turn back. My focus is on one point in the room – a high-backed armchair in the far corner. I throw myself towards it and then reach down for the item I'd hidden behind it.

It's a canister of petrol.

Bending down, I pull it out from behind the chair. I unscrew the cap and then quickly get to work pouring the clear liquid everywhere – over the chairs, over the floor, the table. It glugs out and the acrid smell hits my nostrils.

And then Jesse is upon me.

'Erin, you're going too far! Just stop! Think before you act.'

'I've been thinking about this for years,' I tell him. He tries to wrestle the container away from me but it's too late, it's completely empty.

A shriek goes up from Freya. It cuts right through me. That girl really is annoyingly hysterical.

Jesse is after me again, but I send a well-aimed kick in his direction that is certain to wind him. He doubles over.

I stand on the low coffee table, my shoes getting covered in the petrol. But I don't care. None of it matters any more.

'Erin, please, just think of the children. Do whatever you like to me but don't drag Ophelia and Freya into this.' Nadia sounds distraught. And so she should be. I know she's realised there's no way she can stop me.

I strike the match. The bright orange flame feels strangely soothing.

Faces dance before me: Nadia, Sasha, Jesse, Freya and then Ophelia. I turn my attention away from my daughter and look back at Nadia.

'Say goodbye, everyone.'

The room falls silent. I close my eyes.

I didn't expect this evening to go like this. Then again nothing in my life ever goes to plan and I don't know why I thought this would be any different. But now I understand it has to be this way.

This is how it all ends.

As I blink open my eyes, I let the burning match fall from my hand.

A figure barrels towards me, its solid weight connecting and knocking me to the ground. I'm pretty sure it's Douglas. As sharp pain sears through my head, I see the orange flames whoosh and take hold.

It is done.

I close my eyes for what I hope is the last time.

People may paint me as the villain of this story but I've just never really fitted into this world. I've never understood people or got the rules of relationships. I've perhaps loved too much and my expectations of others to do the same have been too high.

I'm tired of trying to figure it all out. I'm tired of being me.

This is my way out.

I can hear the panicked voices. I can smell the stench of petrol and feel the heat of the fire beginning to take hold in the room. My head is unbearably painful. I want the end to come quickly.

I try to shut out what's going on. In recent years, I've mastered the art of meditation and so I attempt to retreat into my own mind and to concentrate on slipping away into a dreamless state. But it's impossible to do when my body is hurting this much.

Instead, images of Jasper and Ophelia's tiny, little pink faces as babies flood my mind – of them chasing after one another in the lavender fields, of them unwrapping birthday presents by the fireplace.

Jasper and Ophelia. At one time, I thought that having babies might make me a better person. I hoped my children might give me the love I craved. All I ever wanted was to have a family: a husband to love me and children to nurture. If Aaron had been a less controlling husband or if I'd married someone else maybe things would've turned out differently.

Even more memories of my children crash into my thoughts.

And then Ophelia's voice cuts through the space between us.

Ophelia. She's still here in the room.

She's screaming for help.

It was never the original plan to trap my daughter – or any of the children – in this room. Things got out of hand. And I was stunned when Ophelia turned her back on me. But it wasn't her fault and she doesn't deserve to get hurt.

I should've let her go. I should've let them all go. I've done many bad things in my life but this has gone way too far tonight. What kind of monster am I?

If only I'd done things differently.

Could've. Would've. Should've.

A tear rolls down my cheek. I have had a lifetime of hurt and tonight I just snapped. My mind calms. I try to sit, to lever myself up, but my head is heavy and I can't get my legs to move.

I have to get to Ophelia. I try again but I can only drag myself along a few paces.

Ophelia. Save her. Someone please, please save her...

Chapter Thirty-One

Sasha

Everything happens too quickly. One minute Erin is running across the room and the next the overpowering stench of petrol is clogging the air.

She has petrol and matches. And we're trapped. So this is what she was up to.

The flame on the match is bright. I see my husband dive at Erin but I already know it's too late. She wants to kill us all.

I pick Fergus up and put as much distance as I can between us and Erin. Hugging my little boy close, the severity of the situation hits me. We might not get out of here alive. I might not get to see my wonderful, bright, cuddly little child grow up. Dark spots crowd my vision, but I'm not going to give up yet.

I hesitate. I don't know whether to position us by the window or the door. Fergus has buried his head in my shoulder. 'Mummy, please can we go? I don't like that lady.'

If only it were that simple.

I decide the window is the best option. I place Fergus down beside me. Then I yank open the curtains, praying that Hayley might still be on the other side of the window. But she's gone.

Looking behind me, my heart shudders in my chest. The flames are licking up the wood panelling on the far side of the room and one of the sofas is starting to smoulder. I'd never really registered it before, but there's a lot of wood in this room. Covering the walls, floor, furniture. So much fuel for the fire.

My mum and Ophelia have picked up a chair. 'Out of the way!' Nadia commands. They fling the chair at the glass, but it only makes a small crack.

'We need to move faster,' she urges. She picks up the chair by herself and throws it back at the windowpane. The glass cracks a little more this time.

'That's it, Grandma!' Ophelia yells, and then she takes a turn. It's the same result. The glass is cracking but not breaking. If this doesn't work then we might not be able to get out.

The smell of burning materials is filling the air. It's only been a minute since the fire started and this is a big room, with high ceilings, but it won't take long for the space to be engulfed in flames. I think back to the fire safety training I've done for school; we have to do the sessions regularly. Pieces of knowledge slot together in my mind and immediately make me feel more in control.

I remember the advice about covering mouths and noses. This might not help much, but I have to do something. We need to make sure we're not inhaling too much of the toxic air while we're trying to break out. I see a throw on one of the sofas so I reach for it and wrap it tightly around Fergus, in a similar way to how I'd wrap a swimming towel around him. Only his eyes and forehead are poking out of the gap in the fabric.

'Cover your mouths!' I say in a strangled voice to my mother and niece. Nadia at once winds her scarf around the lower part of her face. Ophelia tears a strip out of her dress and fashions a thin makeshift facemask. I'm trying to work out how to protect myself. I go to the curtain but it's too thick.

'Here,' Ophelia shoves another strip of the material of her pink dress at me. Two violent slashes of pink tied to our faces. But all that matters is that we can keep breathing.

With the people nearest to me sorted, my stomach then lurches.

'Where's Freya? And Douglas?' I whip my head around. I'd been expecting them both to appear by my side. I can't see Douglas anywhere. Where is he?

But then I spot Freya. She's stock-still, frozen with fear at the wrong end of the room. I'd been so intent on picking up Fergus and finding a way out, I assumed Freya would follow. Why hasn't she moved?

'Freya!' I scream. 'Run!'

She doesn't budge, her arms hanging limp by her sides. She seems like she's in a trance. Smoke is beginning to swirl close to her and the fire is taking hold. Soon she'll be cut off from the rest of us.

'Don't let go of Fergus,' I instruct my mum. 'I have to get Freya.' I nod to where my daughter is standing.

'Be careful,' she says. Her eyes are watery and I can't tell if it's the effects of the smoke or her emotions. She puts a protective arm around my son.

Ophelia is throwing the chair against the glass again. It's our only hope.

'Freya!' I charge to my daughter. There's a clear path from me to her – until there's not. A burning lamp, complete with ornate lampshade, comes crashing down just inches in front of me, creating a line of fire between me and her.

'I need you to move, Freya,' I urge. 'Move!'

The smoke is becoming more noticeable and I put one arm up in front of my mouth. I can't wait for her to unfreeze, so I jump over the lampshade and hook my arm around my daughter.

'Listen to me Freya, we're going to get down to the other end of the room. Let's focus on that. One step at a time.'

She's completely shut down; she's not responding to me at all. It's as if she's switched off to blot out the chaos that's going on around her.

I guide her along with me. I still can't see Douglas. Flames are multiplying before my eyes in the area where Erin dropped the match and panic grips my heart. I hope to God he isn't over there in it.

'Douglas!' I shout across the room as loud as I can. 'Where are you?'

There's no response but I try to tell myself that he's resourceful and that he will get himself out. I've got to get Freya across the room before she seizes up entirely. If I split my attention, I won't be helping anybody. Her legs are moving stiffly and slowly – I wish I could pick her up like I did with Fergus.

'Put your hand over your mouth,' I instruct her, and she obediently does as I say.

We navigate around the burning lamp. I hold my breath, my chest feeling tight. Just as I think I've got through; the edge of my dress catches alight.

Freya screams at me, pointing at the flaming material. The skin along my leg scorches hot. My eyes go wide. I can't see anything that will put the fire out. I can't think straight, the pain is all-consuming.

Before I can prevent her, Freya reaches for my dress. I try to tell her to stop, but nothing comes out of my mouth.

She rips the heat away from me, the bottom section of the dress tearing. Then she chucks it behind her and claps her hands tightly together to make sure there's no flames left on her skin. Tears are streaming down her cheeks from the excruciating pain.

'Freya, you shouldn't have done that!' I manage to say. My head is swimming but I reach down and slap my leg, making sure there's no more fire on me. As I do so, my palm connects with red, raw skin. I shriek. It hurts like nothing I've ever felt before. Or want to feel again.

There's no time to stop. Another minute has passed and we won't have long left. I can feel the floor getting hot; soon it will be unbearable to walk on. I must keep going. I need to keep Freya and Fergus safe. I need to try and get them out of here.

I cling onto the hope of the emergency services getting to us soon. Someone must have seen the fire or smelt the smoke and alerted the fire brigade. I pray that Hayley has figured out what was going on. If not, there were some other guests staying in the hotel rooms at Burcott House and I'm guessing some staff stay on site overnight as well.

Although it's worrying that I haven't heard a fire alarm yet. The awful thought that Erin may have disabled the alarm when she activated the security lockdown in the building makes me feel sick. I push away the voice in my head telling me that everyone else will be asleep or in their bedrooms because I can't bear to think about the alternative scenario. About what will happen if the blaze isn't noticed soon enough. I have to keep my focus on my children. I'm their mother and they need me. They need me to keep them alive.

Freya loops her arm through mine. I'm not sure who is leaning on whom. Somehow, we manage to push through together. When I look up again, the landscape of the room has changed. There's no-one by the window and the chair that was used to try and smash through the windows is abandoned on the floor. The glass is more battered but not broken.

I left Fergus here with my mother – where are they? Fear catches in my throat. He's too little to fend for himself in this situation. But I had to get to Freya; I couldn't have left her there. I look back at the space where Freya was and it's a wall of smoke. I only just got to her in time.

'Look!' Freya points to the internal door. I can't believe my eyes – it's open! Ophelia is escaping through it, Nadia and Fergus just behind her.

I can see a figure at the door, urging the trio through. It's a man and I don't recognise him. Perhaps it's a firefighter or a police officer? Although it doesn't matter who it is, they're saving us.

Relief floods through me. It's a miracle. We're going to get out. This urges me on and Freya picks up her pace too. But then she stumbles, the bottom of her dress wrapped around the heel of her left shoe. I manage to catch her before she ends up on the floor but she hesitates, grimacing from the pain in her hands.

'Quickly,' I tell her. 'We can be out of here soon. I'll help you.'

She nods and does as I say, wrapping her arm around my shoulder. I grit my teeth and concentrate on supporting her weight to the end of the room, to safety.

Then, just as we're inching closer to our escape route, I see a large section of the ceiling crashing down, almost in slow motion in front of my eyes. My mother and my son dissolve instantly from sight.

A scream rips from my throat. This can't be happening.

We're cut off from our only escape route.

And I have no idea if my mother and my little boy are alive…

Chapter Thirty-Two

Nadia

The ceiling is falling down around me. I react as quickly as I can. Fergus is in my arms; I hold him tight, as we're both half-thrown and half-pulled forward.

Dust and debris whirl around me but my only thought is for the little boy I won't let go of.

'You're OK,' a rough voice says. 'You're okay, you're safe.' Big arms encircle me and I'm pushed through the door and into the next room.

My heart is still beating and my lungs are still pumping hard. I'm still here, I'm still alive. But what about Fergus?

'Darling,' I say as I peel him away from me. 'We're out, it's all alright.'

My grandson is still mostly swaddled in the big throw, only the top of his head peeking out. I drop to my knees, with one arm still around his small body, and I tug the throw off him. He's deathly pale and his legs buckle beneath him.

'There's something wrong,' I say, as I scoop Fergus closer to me so I can prop him up.

Gently, I sweep his fringe away from his face and trace a line down his cheek. He's still breathing but it's too shallow for my liking. I tap his cheek a few times until his eyelids begin to flutter in response. I think he might've fainted but I'm not sure if it's something worse. Maybe he inhaled too much smoke? He's only got little lungs – how much of that poisonous air could he take?

Kissing him on the nose, I watch him squirm slightly and then his eyes fly open. Relief floods through me.

'Where am I?' he says softly.

'You're safe.' I smile faintly at him.

'Thank you...'

I should lay him out on the floor and check him over properly but I'm aware we're still too close to the raging fire and the smoke is beginning to filter through into this room as well. The way the ceiling crashed down right behind us was utterly terrifying – and I'm concerned about the structure of this old building. If we'd been just a footstep slower neither of us would be sitting here right now. Someone pulled us out of harm's way, someone saved our lives. But everything happened at such speed that I have no idea who it was.

Twisting round, I tune into the commotion going on behind me. I clock Leah shouting into the smoky room and then she doubles over, coughing. It catapults me right back into the nightmare again.

She turns to me, still coughing.

My youngest daughter has had bad asthma since she was a child. She needs to get away from there. And then it dawns on me... Leah? Where has she been? Was she in the room when Erin started the fire? I flip back through the last hour. I'm not sure, because everything has been such a blur. She was definitely in the room when Erin reappeared. I can remember the shocked expression on her face when she set eyes on her sister. But after that? I'm not sure...

'Come here, love,' I beckon her to me. 'Help me with Fergus.'

I slap Fergus on the back a few times and he splutters a fair bit. Then, once his airway is cleared, his breathing gets a little better.

'How did you get the door open?' I ask Leah.

'I left the room after Erin took my phone, while everyone was focused on Ophelia. I didn't know exactly what Erin was going to do but I didn't like it. I found Tiana; she'd been waiting for me in the Winchester Room. I told her that Erin was back and something was about to kick off. I just didn't expect this.'

Leah rubs the scar on her face, like she always does when she's nervous. 'We went back and tried the door but it was locked. And then Hayley found us and said she'd seen Erin and the rest of you looked terrified. We rang the police then.'

'Good.' I'm hoping this means it won't be too long until more help arrives. 'Take Fergus,' I tell Leah. 'Get him outside and call the fire brigade.'

'Hayley has already called them,' she informs me. 'And Tiana has been alerting all of the guests staying in rooms, just in case they haven't heard the alarm.'

It's only then I notice the shrill sound of the alarm in the background. It must've just started up.

'You go with Fergus,' she insists.

'No,' I say firmly. 'Your lungs can't take this. I need you out of this building; the most useful thing you can do is get Fergus out of here before the fire spreads.'

'They're all still inside,' Leah protests.

'All?' I blink rapidly.

'Yes, only you, Fergus and Ophelia have come out.'

It feels as though I've been winded. My attention has been solely on my grandson; I'd hoped that the others had followed close behind us.

'Where is Ophelia?' I ask.

'She went with Hayley, to help at the window,' Leah explains. 'Sasha, Freya, Jesse, Douglas and Erin...' She reels off the names. 'They're all still in there.'

'Let's not waste any time,' I say rapidly. 'You take this young lad and make sure he's checked over as soon as an ambulance gets here. Get round to that window, as fast as you can. See if there's something – anything – to break it open. Keep an eye out for what you can use as you go through the building.'

'There's something else I have to tell you,' Leah garbles.

'There's no time,' I say firmly. There's nothing more important than getting my family out of that room.

Leah seems uncertain but she gives me a brief hug and then picks Fergus up. She races towards the exit and I wish I could follow her, away from this nightmare, but I must make sure my daughters and granddaughter get out of that inferno.

I turn and prepare myself to dive back into the hellish room.

And then I gasp.

Because I understand what Leah wanted to tell me. Standing in the doorframe is my ex-husband. Craig Turner.

He's back. All the dots begin to join. All those questions: who helped Erin? Where has she been? Why didn't she make contact? They all point to one answer.

It was him. Craig must've had something to do with it.

Now here he is, standing in between me and the people I love most in the world.

'Nadia,' he springs towards me, his mouth set in a grim line.

I put my hands up in front of me, warning him to keep his distance. My body trembles because I have no idea what he's about to do. Has my ex-partner come back for revenge? Is he working with Erin? Does he want us all dead too?

All these things are possible. After all, I stitched him up and testified against him. He went back to jail for Xavier Knight's murder because of me. The jury believed every word I said about him, although they didn't take much convincing because he'd served two murder sentences already. When he stood in the dock, everyone saw a man who had killed before and so they didn't believe anything that came out of his mouth.

I was the liar though. I did what was necessary to keep this man away from my family.

'Get away from me!' I scream at him. I've dreaded the day I came face to face with him again. Eighteen months ago, he managed to escape when he was being transferred between prisons. No-one has seen or heard of him since.

'Nadia, it was me. I pulled you out of the room.' Craig's voice is level and not at all threatening.

'You?' Confusion clouds my mind. 'Why?'

Craig seems smaller than I remember him. He's lost weight and is slightly hunched over. There's a grey pallor to his face as well. He looks ill.

I shake my head; we can't have this conversation now. 'Just move. Freya is still in there. She's too young to...'

I can't finish my sentence but the look on Craig's face tells me he gets exactly what I was going to say.

'You can't go back in there. I've just tried. It's too dangerous.'

I don't even answer him, I just push him aside.

'I mean it, Nadia; you can't see anything. It's impossible.'

I refuse to believe him. For all I know, he's in on this with Erin and it's all part of some big master plan. I wind the scarf back round my face and then go to step back into the room, but Craig grasps my arm.

'No Nadia, I'm not losing you.'

'You lost me half a lifetime ago,' I snap back at him, before stepping back into the room.

To my dismay, Craig's right. I can barely see a few paces in front of me. There's a roaring noise that fills my ears as I try not to inhale. I cast around wildly and see the section where the ceiling fell down, only a few paces in front of me. I think I can make out a figure by the window on the far side of the room, but I'm not sure.

Craig is then by my side; he grasps my hand and I don't pull away. I'm scared. It's too much, I need fresh oxygen. He barrels me back out of the room but when we go back through to the bar area next door, the air quality isn't much better.

'We need to get out of here,' Craig says urgently.

Something creaks and groans. I'm terrified the ceiling will crumble above us.

'I can't leave them,' I'm sobbing.

'Let's go outside and try getting them out of the window.'

I'm about to argue when there's an almighty crash behind us. Something tips through the doorway; it's the wooden coat stand that was positioned next to the entrance to the snug. It falls into the space we're in.

'The whole house is going to go up.' Craig curses. He picks up the throw that had been wrapped around Fergus and covers the coat stand. It acts like a tea towel over a saucepan and the flames are extinguished.

'That's not going to stop it for long,' he mutters. 'We should shut the door, to stop it spreading.'

'If we shut the door then it'll be harder for them to get out,' I argue.

I see the expression on his face and it makes me want to scream.

'You think they're all already dead, don't you?'

'I...' he stutters, clearly not expecting the question.

'Don't you?' I demand.

'I hope not. You're right; let's leave the door open to give them an escape route. We need to get outside to the window. That's where we can help the most.'

Hesitating, I wait one more moment, willing at least one person to emerge out of the room. Nothing happens. I reluctantly allow Craig to sweep me along with him, moving as fast as our bodies will allow. We exit through the Winchester Room, which is completely untouched, looking just as it did when we were in here an hour ago. How is that possible?

I'm hot and sweaty, my brain even feels like it's on fire. I'm finding it hard to process everything. There are five people still in the snug. Whatever they've done, whatever they've said, I don't want any one of them perishing tonight.

I try to picture where they were all standing. Sasha had gone to get Freya. Erin, Douglas and Jesse were all in the thick of it on the other side of the room. I try to wipe the images from my mind. It's not helping, it's just slowing me down.

As we move through Burcott House, I fling questions at Craig. 'How did you get the door open? Erin said the house was in security lockdown. Or did the fire disable it?'

'It was me, I lifted the lockdown,' Craig puffs back. 'I knew Erin was coming back here, to confront you all. I just didn't believe she would go this far.'

'You've been together, the pair of you, haven't you? Where've you been hiding? Have you been camped out in Rio de Janeiro with Ronnie Biggs's family?'

'Erin broke me out of jail; she's very resourceful. I was proud of her to begin with but that girl is dangerous.'

I want to ask more but it'll have to wait. We hurry outside. Fresh air hits me and I inhale big, deep lungfuls of it. The clean air us humans take for granted, and yet it is one of the essentials for life. Outside, I take the lead. Craig doesn't know Burcott House as well as I do. We skirt around the edge of the property; it feels like it's taking forever to reach the window where the snug is but in reality, it's just a few seconds.

Finally, I see the knot of people by the window. It spurs me on. We pass Leah who is sitting with Fergus on a bench, away from the scene that's unfolding. Fergus has his head buried in Leah's armpit and she's singing soothing songs to him. I'm relieved to see his breathing looks normal.

'I feel useless,' Leah says to me.

'You've done everything you can. Look, there's no need for Fergus to be this close. Take him to the front and wait for the emergency services.'

As I say this a siren wail cuts through the air.

'Thank goodness!' I exclaim. I just hope they're not too late.

Leah jumps up and, pulling Fergus onto her hip, she spirits him away with her in the direction of the reinforcements.

Craig and I keep going. Hayley comes into view. There's glass on the ground and a heavy, concrete garden ornament cracked in two.

Adrenalin rushes through me. They did it! They smashed through the window.

Emerging through the broken shards of the window is Freya. Sasha is passing her over to Hayley. Craig runs full pelt and helps Hayley lift Freya out onto the grass. Her body is floppy as they move her. Hayley rapidly starts administering CPR.

'She's not in a good way,' Hayley is muttering.

'The ambulance has just arrived.' I say, trying to reassure myself as much as Hayley.

Hayley nods but she's concentrating on counting as she tries to get the blood pumping around Freya's body.

I have to turn away. I don't know what to do in this situation, I can't watch while my Freya is so still. Hayley is a teaching assistant as well as a Brownie leader, and I know that she's had medical training to deal with emergencies like this. She will do all she can for my granddaughter and I take comfort in knowing the professionals are also here – I can see them spilling out across the grass, coming to help us. Moving out of the way, I tell myself that Freya will be in the best possible hands. She has to pull through, she has to.

Everything feels unreal. This is really happening but my brain can't process it. I switch my attention back to the house. Sasha is still on the window ledge, half in and half out. One of her legs is an angry shade of red.

But what is she doing?

Craig and Sasha are tussling between them. Coming level with them, I hear Craig cursing Sasha. Then, in one heart-stopping instant, Sasha disappears back inside the burning room...

Chapter Thirty-Three

Craig

'What did you just do?' Nadia half-screams at me.

'Me?' She's got the wrong idea about what just happened. 'I was trying to stop her but she wouldn't listen to me.'

Sasha has gone entirely from view. My pulse races.

'Why has she gone back in?' Nadia is wringing her hands as she speaks.

'She said she knows where Douglas is.'

Nadia rubs her forehead agitatedly. 'She's going to kill herself trying to get him out of there.'

Ducking my head in through the gap in the brickwork, I try to peer inside but the room is thick with smoke. The time has been ticking by; I'm guessing it must be at least five minutes since the fire started, and I fear that Sasha has pushed her luck too far.

Then Sasha's back again, bent towards us, her head out of the window, rasping and trying to suck in as much air as she can.

'Get her out, whatever it takes,' Nadia pleads. I'm surprised she's asking for my help, but I have every intention of trying to manoeuvre our wilful daughter to safety.

Acting immediately, I hook my hands under Sasha's armpits. She resists, which I was expecting. I try again. There's less fight in her;

she's getting tired, losing energy. I pull her unceremoniously out of the window. It's not easy as she starts to kick and flail. I'm aware I'm dragging her across the shards of glass but that's the least of our worries.

Sasha lashes out again and we both topple over and fall on the downtrodden grass. She attempts to push herself up but flops back down again. She can barely speak but she's croaking out words, her face filled with fear.

'What is it?'

'Douglas,' she stammers. 'I got him. He's so close to the window. He was just... too heavy.'

Suddenly, a member of the ambulance crew is upon us, gathering Sasha up and firing questions at me. I just say very loudly and clearly, 'There are three people in that room. Two men and one woman. One of the men is near the window.'

'We can't go in,' the kindly paramedic says calmly. 'But the firefighters will be on the scene soon.' The woman bends down to check Sasha. Sasha looks exhausted, but at least she's alive.

Scanning the gardens, I see the red fire engine beyond the fence in the car park. It's going to be a good few minutes before they reach the snug. Those few minutes could be the difference between life and death for at least one of the people inside.

'I'm going in,' I announce. 'I'll get Douglas out. And I'll find Erin.'

'I'll come with you.' Nadia is right behind me.

'No, Nadia. There are people out here who need you.' I nod in Freya's direction. My granddaughter has thankfully responded to the CPR. She rolls onto one side and then heaves up the contents of her stomach.

'Go to them.' I give Nadia a small smile as I gesture towards Sasha and Freya.

I've longed to be with Nadia again since we last parted. I messed everything up between us. If I'd just behaved, kept my nose clean, maybe gone to work in a factory or on a building site instead of chasing fortune, then we might still be together. Maybe we'd be enjoying our retirement with long country walks and weekends by the sea. I like to think in a parallel universe, there's a version of us doing just that. Perhaps our daughters are all friends after having a nice, stable, ordinary upbringing. But that wasn't the path I chose, and I need to make amends for that.

'Craig,' Nadia places a hand on my arm. 'Be careful.' She quickly unwinds her scarf and gives it to me. 'Put this on,' she instructs.

Accepting the scarf, I nod my thanks. Then I take one last look at the world around me. Sasha is sitting upright and she's breathing normally. At least one of my daughters has survived this. Freya is being carried on a stretcher to a waiting ambulance but the paramedics aren't rushing, which makes me think she'll be OK. Ophelia is with Freya, walking alongside her. They made it. For once, I did something good and I feel proud. If only I'd discovered this feeling earlier on in my life.

'Go,' I whisper to Nadia. And she does, turning away from me and back to her girls. I watched her walk away over and over but it never got any easier at the end of each prison visit. This time it hurts more because I'm sure I won't see her again.

I don't falter as I slide back into the room. The smoke hits me and I know how risky this is but I plough on anyway. The scarf around my face smells of Nadia and I try to focus on this instead of the stench of burning materials. The air is toxic, I keep my mouth shut tight. That's not the only challenge. Everything is too hot: the ground beneath my feet, the walls, the furniture. I try not to touch anything but it's hard to see.

Sasha said Douglas was near the window so I concentrate on trying to find him first. I trip and almost fall over a chair but manage to right myself. I cast around but find nothing. I quickly dip my head back out into the night air and breathe deeply. Then I twist back and refocus on my mission.

I drop down to the floor and I find something, to the left of the window. The shape of a body. The smoke is heavy I can't see who it is. I bend down and put my arms around the torso. I don't even attempt to speak because I need to save my breath and it's clear that the person on the ground isn't moving. I heave them into a sitting position, but they're a deadweight and unresponsive. I can tell it's a man now and I guess it's Douglas, given Sasha's description of where she left him. He's bigger than me so it's not easy but I manage to drag him closer to the window.

My lungs are screaming, I want to dip back out for more air but this person is in a much worse state than me so I need to get him out fast. I hoist him up and I'm relieved to see a firewoman is on the other side of the gap. She helps me to lift the lifeless form out of the window.

'Douglas!' Sasha breathlessly joins us. 'Oh, it's him! You found him, thank you! Thank you!' She kisses me on the cheek while I'm still half in and half out of the window.

'I did it for you, my daughter.'

She doesn't hear me; she's already turned her attention to her husband as two members of the ambulance crew get to work on pumping his chest. He's covered in black soot and I don't fancy his chances of survival.

Nadia is with me; her hands clasp mine. She heard what I said even if Sasha didn't. 'That was a brave thing to do,' she says sincerely.

'It was necessary. I owe that girl.'

Tears well in Nadia's eyes. She has a silver foil blanket around her shoulders and she looks smaller and more vulnerable than I've ever seen her before. One of the reasons I fell in love with her was her strength of character, which I know is still there despite everything she's been through in her life.

'I'm going to find Erin,' I say softly. It's what I have to do.

Nadia looks at me sadly. 'She could already be gone.'

She's right, but I've got to try. I need to know if Erin is still alive.

An older firefighter, with deep lines on his face, comes over to us. 'Sir, let's get you out,' he says urgently. 'You've done a heroic job but you need to look after yourself now.'

It's very tempting just to obey and do what I'm being told to do. I could easily step away and enjoy whatever is left of my life. But I've never been very good at following the rules and I've always acted on impulse, even though it's usually landed me in trouble.

'My daughter is still in there,' I say.

'I'm sorry but we've been assessing the situation. It's not safe to go back in, we have to make this call.' He repeats, 'I'm sorry.'

I allow him to heave me onto the grass away from the window ledge. I need to catch my breath and think. Nadia sits next to me, tears streaming down her face. Once the firefighter is satisfied that I'm clear of the building, he jogs back to his team, who are getting closer. I can see them setting up the water hoses on their way.

'I thought I'd lost her once already.' Nadia's eyes mist. 'Now I'm losing her all over again.'

Is it true? Would Erin really have perished in there so quickly?

'What happened anyway? How did the fire start?' I ask, breathing slowly and deeply. My mind is numb. The firefighter said no one could be alive in there, but is he right?

'It was Erin,' Nadia confesses. 'She had a canister of petrol and a match. I still don't understand why she did it…'

I expected this answer and Nadia has just confirmed it for me. Erin was responsible. I'm not surprised. It turns out my daughter is even more of a criminal than I am. But it's over now and there are things I need to say.

'You have a right to know what happened after Erin vanished from the mountainside. Erin had a burner phone on her and she contacted Marnie for help.'

Nadia's head shakes slowly. 'Ah. The dots finally connect. I always wondered if Marnie might have been involved.'

Marnie, the woman who owned the ski chalet in the French Alps opposite to Erin's, had harboured Erin in a remote house in the French countryside and nursed her to recovery. The police caught up with me and I went straight back to jail. I did twelve months for breaking my original bail conditions and then I was also convicted me for the murder of Xavier Knight at the ski resort.

Xavier was one of Erin's family friends and Leah had been close to starting a relationship with him. It honestly wasn't a murder I committed but I was a twice-convicted killer, freshly released from prison, and Nadia testified against me. She told an entire courtroom that she'd seen me murder Xavier. It was flimsy evidence but, given my track record, I didn't have a chance. I'd already spent most of my adult life locked away. I don't blame Nadia for what she did, I understand she felt she was protecting her family and maybe she did believe I was dangerous.

They also tried to convict me for the deaths of Shane and Lindsay Robertson, the married Australian couple whose bodies were found on the mountaintop weeks after Xavier's murder, as well as questioning me about Erin's disappearance. There wasn't enough evidence for those crimes but they threw the book at me and gave me another twenty-five-year sentence for Xavier's death. I was told I'd spend the rest of my life behind bars.

And I nearly did.

'Yes, Marnie and Erin broke me out of jail eighteen months ago. It worked, thanks to a very corrupt prison officer who, for a price, turned a blind eye during my transfer between prisons. A team of ex-cons, organised by Erin, smuggled me out of the van.'

'Ah!' Nadia exclaims. 'I obviously knew you'd escaped; it was all over the news. I wondered who had helped you get out.'

'Well now you know. From there I went to Ireland and on to Europe.'

Nadia interrupts me again. 'I was trying to keep tabs on you. I even hired a private investigator to try and find your whereabouts. He tracked you to Ireland and then France – which was further than the police got – but after that there was nothing.'

'Erin's clever. She'd been hiding for all this time and had learnt a few tricks. Hiding me as well was easy for her. I've been living in Croatia for the last year with Erin and Marnie. To begin with, it was like I'd landed in paradise. I've never been anywhere so beautiful. The sea was sparkling, the sun was always shining. I would've been content to live out my days there.' I speak quickly because I want Nadia to hear the truth.

I pause for breath and then go on. 'Except Erin's behaviour was obsessive. All she thought about was the family she had left behind and the ways in which she'd wanted to fully punish everyone. She had this grand plan that involved both me and Jesse coming back here to Burcott House. She wanted the whole family to be under one roof when she revealed herself to still be alive. She told me she wanted to take her children back but, the closer we got to the date, the more erratic and unstable her behaviour became. I sensed there was more to it than she was letting on.'

Nadia pinches the bridge of her nose. I remember her doing this when we lived together and she was frustrated with me. Which was often.

'She's sharp and nothing I did to try and stop her worked, so I came with her and I hoped that once she'd seen Jasper and Ophelia her feelings might change. She must've realised I was trying to derail her plans as she abandoned me – shoved me out of the car on the way here. I was lost in the countryside for a bit but I found my way to Burcott House in the end. I'm glad I did, otherwise that house would still be locked tight and perhaps no-one would've got out alive.'

'How did Erin turn out like this?' Nadia's eyes are on the blazing room behind us. 'How could she do it?'

The heat behind me is intense and I can see the older firefighter coming back towards us. He'll try to move us away from the building but there's something I need to do first.

'Look Nadia, I know what I am and what I've done. But, as black as my heart is, I never stopped loving my family. I never stopped loving you...'

Nadia hangs her head, avoiding eye contact. I never expected her to jump back into my arms. Not after everything I put her through, especially after I pulled strings from prison to ensure that her partner Simon met with a fatal accident. I've always regretted that. I thought she might make peace with me in some way if I aired my feelings but she continues to look steadily at the ground, refusing to meet my gaze.

'It's OK, you don't have to say anything. I've chosen the wrong path and I've wasted my life. But I'm going to try to set things right.'

Nadia is about to say something, but a scream rips through the night. It's bloodcurdling and doesn't sound human but there's no doubt that it's coming from inside the building.

'Someone is still alive in there! I'm not taking any chances.'

'What do you mean?'

'Erin lost all sense of reality. She's more dangerous than any criminal I've ever known, and that's saying something! I'm getting closer to my judgement day, so I'm doing the one last thing I can for this family. I'm going back in there.'

'The fire officer just said no-one could survive this.'

'I'm not going in to save Erin. I'm going in to make sure she doesn't come out.'

'Craig, don't do it,' Nadia cries. 'Save her! Don't let her die in there, whatever she's done, bring her back to me.'

Shaking my head, I say, 'I'm doing this for the rest of you. While Erin lives and breathes none of you are safe.'

Nadia reaches out for me but I get up quickly, moving out of her grasp.

'I love you,' I say softly. Then I swiftly pull my wallet out of my back pocket, flip it open and place it in her hand. The photograph facing upwards is the first one we ever took of the two of us. We both look fresh-faced and young. Nadia is laughing and I'm kissing her cheek. The photo is faded and worn but our happiness is still plain to see.

'You kept this?' Nadia whispered.

'Always. It's yours now.'

Before she can say anything else, I throw myself back through the window. I hear the shouts of the fire brigade behind me but I don't listen to them.

I lurch forward, knowing I'm going to die. The idea doesn't scare me. Unlike Nadia, there's no-one who really needs me or will miss me. I've considered death a lot lately, especially since I've been getting the pains in my chest. I don't need a doctor to tell me that my heart is failing. The idea of months of slow, agonising decline frightens me more than walking through flames.

A scream bounces around the room and I head in the direction of it. There's another small window in the snug. It's been broken and air is coming through it. For a heartbeat, I think Erin has already escaped but the window is too high up for anyone to climb out of. Debris is falling all around me and I realise I might be crushed before I discover the fate of my devious daughter.

I trip over a prone figure on the floor. It's Jesse. He's lying stretched out at Erin's feet. She is in an upright foetal position, her head tucked into her bent knees. The area she's sitting in is strangely wet. Then, through the smoky air, I see the open fridge in the corner. Bottles and bottles of water have been emptied in an attempt to douse the flames. It's slowed things down in this area of the room but it won't prevent the inevitable.

Jesse has remained by Erin's side and Erin has fought to do everything she could to survive. Sadness stabs my heart. I wish I didn't have to do this, but I've got to protect the others. As long as Erin is alive, there's no telling what she'll do.

Erin doesn't lift her head. I'm not sure if she's already gone. I sit down beside her and I see her legs have been badly scorched. Her breathing is laboured and she's wheezing, clinging onto life.

'It's me, it's your dad,' I tell her.

'Is Ophelia alive?' Erin manages to stutter.

Her question surprises me – maybe she regrets her actions. 'Yes, Ophelia is safe.'

'Good... I never meant to harm my baby.'

Erin exhales but then coughs as she breathes back in. I'm finding it harder to breathe too, and I'm starting to feel quite dizzy. Have I done the wrong thing? Is Erin sorry for what she's done?

'And the rest of them, are they all dead?'

The icy way she says this gives me the answer I need. Erin wouldn't stop until she'd achieve what she set out to do. I was right; no member of the Bailey family will be safe with her still alive.

This has to happen like this.

Erin coughs over and over again until finally her breathing becomes even shallower. I'm expecting her to try one last attempt to survive. Instead, she slumps against me.

I kiss her gently on the forehead before placing my arm around her and gathering her to me. I haven't got much right in my life but I know this is the right way to finish things. I hold my daughter tightly to me.

And we'll stay like this until the end.

Chapter Thirty-Four

Nadia

I get the sickening feeling that I shouldn't have let Craig go. As much heartache as that man has caused me over my lifetime, I don't want him to get hurt in there. Although I knew nothing that I said would make him listen to me. The question is, will he save our daughter or will he go down in flames with her? I'm still so close, the smoke clogging in the air outside is beginning to sting my eyes. I desperately want Craig to pull Erin out but I'm also afraid of the consequences if she did emerge from the snug. My heart and my head are saying different things, just like that terrible moment at the edge of the mountain.

The words of the Tarot reader come back to me: 'The Devil... and Death.' I remember the image of The Tower card with the flames licking the windows. The Tarot reader, who I briefly mistook for Erin, said The Tower card was standing out to her most and she was certainly right about the fire. On the image of the tower, there were two figures falling through the air. Did that mean anything? Will more than one person meet their end tonight? Jesse, Erin and Craig are all still in there – will any of them survive?

'Madam, can you get away from there,' a stern fire officer shouts, marching in my direction.

I can't move. I'm rooted to the spot. The enormity of what's happening hits me like a punch to the stomach. The minute I step away from here, that's it. My part in this is over. I may never get to see my middle child again. Memory after memory crashes through my mind. The first time I held Erin and the way she scrunched up her little nose; her confidence, even at five years old, as she ran into the classroom on her first day of school, her copper-coloured pigtails flying behind her; the day of her first dance show when she took centre stage, her head held high; an image of her ripping open a doll she'd wanted on Christmas Day; how beautiful she looked at her school prom, in an emerald-green dress.

These are happy moments with my bold, daring little girl that I will never forget. I wish I could stop the bad memories following but they come thick and fast too: Erin and I arguing on the stairs in our terrace house; Erin's ghostly pale face after the car accident when she knocked down Leah; watching her sinister smile as her husband Aaron fell to his death; her screams on the mountainside where I thought she'd died. I walked away from her once to protect the rest of my family but it was the hardest thing I've ever done. I can't do it again.

There's no way I can leave. I can't just turn away knowing that Erin and Craig are still in that death-trap of a room.

'Erin! Erin, I'm coming for you,' I shout out, launching myself half way through the opening in the window.

Except I don't get very far. A firm hand grasps hold of my upper arm. 'No, Mum. It's too dangerous.'

Sasha is yanking me out of the window. I hadn't been aware of her returning to me. Our roles have reversed; not long ago she was bolting into the building to get to Douglas. I can't believe she's stopping me from doing the same and a jolt of red-hot anger shoots through me.

'Let me go!' I pant, 'They need me.'

'It's too late,' she repeats.

I know what she's saying is probably true but a madness has taken hold of me. I thrash against her, screaming Erin's name. I've tried to be strong and to do what's best for my family but I've lived with the guilt of walking away from my middle child for the last ten years and I can't do it again.

'Mum, if I thought there was any chance, I'd go back in there with you. Jesse – the father of my first-born...' Sasha's voice wobbles. 'I don't want it to end like this but there's nothing we can do. Erin...'

She trails off and her visible emotion makes me pause. The fight goes out of me. I've always tried to stay strong for my family but this has pushed me past my limit. My head is thumping and my throat is raw from screaming. Sasha's arm circles around me as she tries to move me but I can't move a muscle, let alone put one foot in front of the other.

The notion this is all my fault keeps circling my mind. I'm Erin's mother. Am I to blame for the awful things she's done? Did I do something wrong? I shouldn't have been so hard on her when she fell for Jesse. It was a teenage crush; it probably would've fizzled out in a few weeks had it run its natural course. Instead, we've had decades of family problems and too many years where we haven't had any kind of relationship.

Maybe if I'd still been in her life, things would've been different. Maybe we could've avoided all of this pain. *Maybe, maybe, maybe.*

My vision is blurred with tears. I stagger and expect to feel my body hitting the ground. But someone breaks my fall. Someone bigger and taller than Sasha. I wonder if the figure is Craig. Has he escaped? Has he rescued Erin? Blinking rapidly and calming myself, I come back to reality. But it's not Craig with his arms around me, it's a burly police officer. The police have arrived as well and the gardens of Burcott House, only hours ago filled with smiling people drinking wine, are crawling with emergency services.

'Come with me,' the officer half-lifts me a few steps and it's impossible to resist the direction he's propelling me in.

Sasha leads me away from Burcott House; the police officer is on the other side of me. It's obvious they don't trust me and I don't blame them, I don't trust myself either. As I put one foot in front of the other, I can feel my whole body shaking. My legs are like jelly and, after a few more paces, they can't hold my weight. I sink to the grass, sobs wracking through me. I don't think I've ever felt sadness like this. It's overwhelming.

'Mum, the firefighters are doing the best they can,' Sasha says gently. 'Let's get out the way and let them do their job with the hoses.'

Lifting my head, I meet her gaze.

'Don't try to go back. I need you. We all need you.' The look she gives me finally jolts me out of my spiralling thoughts. I think of my precious family: Freya, Fergus, Douglas, Leah, Ophelia and Jasper. The six people who are my world. I love them all whole-heartedly and my goal in the past few years has been to keep them safe and happy. That hasn't changed so I must carry on for them.

Nodding, I allow Sasha and the police officer to help me up.

'Are you OK?' the police officer asks.

'I'm fine.' I'm the furthest I've ever been from fine but the answer trips off my tongue as it's the answer he's looking for.

Sasha and the police officer talk over my head, like I'm a child, and then, once he's satisfied that I'm no longer a risk, he strides off towards one of the police vehicles. His walkie-talkie crackles as he goes. It's only then I take in how much activity there is going on around me. Countless firefighters are setting off jets of water to douse the blaze. Sasha tells me it was difficult for them to reach the snug and some of the crew have gone in through the front of the hotel where they're working to put the fire out. But I fear they will be too late for Erin and Craig.

Leaning on Sasha, she directs me to the car park where another ambulance is waiting. I can't look back at Burcott House. I will never, ever step foot in that building ever again because, in my heart, I think I know what the outcome of tonight is going to be.

Chapter Thirty-Five

Ophelia

Smoke rises into the night air, the fire spreading to the upstairs floors. Leah and I are huddled together on the lawn of Burcott House as flames leap upwards. We're watching, waiting, wondering what will happen next. All of it feels unreal: Jesse returning, seeing my mother strike that match, and coming so close to death in that scorching hot room.

My muscles are tight with tension and my head is still throbbing from my fall earlier this evening. I'm worried about Freya – she looked grey when the paramedics lifted her into the ambulance. I wanted to go with her but I also needed to be here to see if my mum survives this. Leah promised she'd stay with me while Sasha and my grandmother decided they'd be the ones to go to the hospital. Sasha wanted to be with Freya, of course, but Douglas was also in a bad way. It was obvious the pair of them didn't want me going in the ambulances in case something bad happens to him.

Hayley is looking after Fergus. She and her husband Andrew have taken him with their little girls to the nearest hotel. He was asleep for much of the night so fingers crossed he won't remember everything, but the poor thing is going to be scarred for life after being trapped in that room. We all are.

'I can't stand this,' I whisper to Leah.

'Neither can I,' she admits. 'The waiting is horrible. We don't have to stay. It's not like we can do anything.'

Shaking my head, I say, 'I can't leave. If they bring her out and she's... awake... I want to see her.'

I'm sure Leah would much rather leave than be here in the middle of the night waiting for bad news. I fold my arms, hugging them around me. I have to know if my mum is alive or dead. I don't know how I'll react either way. My thoughts about my mum are in turmoil after the events of tonight. I hate her for starting this fire, for putting us all in danger. But do I really want her to die?

More minutes go by and there's still no sign of her or Jesse. Leah told me that Craig went back into the room. I don't understand why – the fire service had already turned up. Although, it was down to him that Douglas got lifted out. He may have saved his life. I've never really given my grandfather much thought. I only met him that one time at the ski chalet when I was a little girl. Now, I'm praying for him to walk out of that building. He saved Douglas so he deserves another chance.

All of a sudden, there's a lot of activity – loud shouts from the fire crew. I really hope that none of them get injured trying to sort out my mum's mess. I would never, ever have spoken to her and got involved in her scheme to organise the party if I'd known the night was going to end up like this. I shouldn't have gone stirring up the past. I feel like everything that's happened tonight is all my fault.

'What do you think is going on?' I ask Leah.

She shrugs. Her eyes are gritty with tiredness.

We watch from a distance as the flames finally start to die down. The fire crew are getting it under control. My eyes are glued to the activity as we see firefighters go into the room that was once the snug. I notice an ambulance has driven over the lawn, leaving deep tyre marks in the previously pristine grass, pulling up closer to Burcott House.

I exhale. 'Do you think someone is alive? And that's why the ambulance has gone up there?'

'I'm not sure,' Leah says, rubbing her temples.

I crane my neck and keep my eyes locked on the window to the snug. Two firefighters bring a body out on a stretcher, covered in a blanket. Just seconds later, the same thing happens and another covered body is being carried out on a stretcher. I've seen enough detective shows to know what a body being covered up means.

There are two bodies there, but who are they? Jesse? Craig? Or Erin?

And where's the third one?

Time ticks by very slowly. The two bodies are taken into the ambulance. There are no more stretchers and the firefighters are turning their attention back to putting out the rest of the blaze.

After what feels like an eternity, a police officer marches in our direction. I stay where I am, steeling myself for whatever we are about to be told.

Leah puts her arm around my shoulders. 'I'm here for you,' she says softly.

But I can't reply, my mouth has gone dry.

The officer reaches us and I notice he has his cap in his hand.

'Leah Bailey and Ophelia Bailey-Scott?' His strong London accent seems out of place in the countryside but perhaps I'm fixating on small details because, one way or another, the information he has to share will change my family forever.

We nod in unison.

'I have some news...'

Epilogue, Part One
Nadia

One month later

We all file out of the church. My black, patent shoes crunch on the gravel beneath my feet. I hate these shoes because they rub the backs of my ankles but also because they're the shoes I always wear to funerals. A witness to my grief.

I've shed so many tears in the last few weeks. Tears of anger, pain and sadness. There will be many more to come. I'm not sure how I'm going to get through the next part of the funeral but I have to do it.

We trudge along the path towards the memorial garden and I pull the brim of my wide hat down to cover more of my face. I'm glad I did this because, seconds later, I hear the tell-tale click of a camera. There's no need to look sideways, as I already know there will be journalists crowding by the hedge that runs along the edge of the cemetery. Our family has once again become the focus of a media storm.

Stories about Aaron's death and Erin's disappearance ten years ago have been rehashed and recirculated. Every detail of the fire at Burcott House has been guessed at and written about. I released a public statement a week ago to ask for privacy for my family at this difficult time but no-one has taken any notice of it. In fact, the interest has just intensified in the days leading up to the funeral.

I'm aware of two police officers – sent here to make sure things don't get out of hand – going over to the merciless photographers and reporters who are trying to get the scoop on the tragic event playing out today.

We reach the burial plot and it suddenly dawns on me that a burial may not have been the wisest choice, given the circumstances. Will this grave become a beacon for true crime podcasters and ghost tours? Although the alternative would have been a cremation and, after the fire, there was no way I could've gone ahead with that option.

'Hey,' Hayley takes my arm as we come to a stop. 'How are you holding up?'

'As you'd expect.' I give her a watery smile. 'Thank you for coming.'

Hayley, Andrew and Ophelia are the only other people here today. None of the rest of my family wanted to attend, which is understandable, and because of the excessive media interest we decided not to open the invite to friends or extended family.

Andrew is on my other side and I feel grateful to have this caring couple to support me. Ophelia is a few paces away from us, having made it clear she wants some space. I'm aware of the police officers bustling around us and then realise they're putting up a black screen. I'm shocked that it's required but also relieved that we're being screened off so that the paparazzi can't get pictures of the coffins going into the ground.

Their scrutiny is intense because today we're burying multiple members of the Bailey family. One body sells a good amount of news stories but more deaths equal more sales. And that's exactly what the journalists have got in the aftermath of the fire at Burcott House.

'We have come together to bury...' the elderly vicar begins '... Craig Turner.'

Silent tears fall down my cheeks, for all that has been lost and all that could've been. Hayley passes me a fresh tissue and I dab my eyes. I've spent most of my life hating Craig Turner. Firstly, I hated him for leaving me alone, as a single mother, when he first went to prison. Then I hated him for being the father of my children when my children's other friends had reliable, present fathers. Later, I hated him more than ever when he arranged the accident that killed my beloved Simon.

But to begin with I did love Craig, passionately. I remember those first few months of us being together and then I picture him clearly as he told me he loved me at Burcott House for the last time. I can't go on hating Craig any more. He was misguided and he made many terrible mistakes but he didn't exactly have the best role models in life. He was destined for a life of crime. Then, in the end, he tried to do what he believed was right.

'Let us pray...' the vicar is saying. My mind is all over the place and I can't concentrate properly but I'm here to say goodbye. To get closure.

My eyes dart over to Ophelia. Her hands are clasped in front of her and she's staring at the ground, lost in thought. I'm concerned today will be too much for her but she was adamant she wanted to come and, for some people, going to a funeral is what they need during the grieving process.

'We also lay to rest the ashes of Jesse Bailey...'

In a way it's ironic that Jesse took the Bailey surname when he married Sasha. Perhaps he also took on some kind of curse of bad luck along with the name, because Jesse's body didn't survive the fire. I didn't ask for the details, but the hospital crematorium gave us his ashes. Neither Sasha nor Freya could face coming to the funeral. Freya is still fragile, although recovering well, and Sasha has been at Douglas's side night and day. I can understand her not wanting to be away from her husband.

I wipe my brow. It's a pleasantly warm day but I'm far too hot in this outfit. And just thinking about the last few weeks makes me feel clammy. Douglas's recovery has not been straightforward. It was touch-and-go in the week after the fire and he was very close to dying. The doctor informed Sasha that if he'd been in the smoke-filled room any longer it would've killed him. Sasha has been beating herself up for not getting him out sooner but she did what she could. No-one knows how they would react in such a high-pressure, life-or-death moment until they're in that situation. She helped get him closer to safety and Craig then saved his life.

Douglas also made a confession to Sasha. He told her that he and Jesse were fighting, throwing punches as the flames first whooshed along the line of petrol Erin had poured. That fight cost Jesse his life and it looks like it's cost Douglas his long-term health.

But that wasn't all. Douglas told Sasha he understood why she had kicked out at Erin on the mountainside. He too had done something to protect himself and his family. He knocked Jesse out cold. That meant Jesse wasn't able to save himself while Douglas – a good, kind man – has had his world changed forever. He will have to live with that burden on his shoulders. Sasha and I decided it was best not to let

Freya know what happened. But I have vowed it will be the last secret the Bailey women keep...

Clasping my hands together, I think about how Craig's and Jesse's deaths have hit the family in different ways. Freya has been beside herself with grief. Losing her father has hit her hard. Leah has been a lot more subdued than I anticipated – she's been rocked by Jesse's death too. They used to be such close friends. Craig's passing has affected me more than anyone but it's also changed the shape of the Bailey family. Someone who had been there, always in the background, but there, is now gone.

'And, finally, we bury the body of Erin Bailey-Scott...'

These were the words I was dreading today. A mother should never have to bury her child. My stomach flips and I wipe my eyes with a tissue once more. Erin had become unrecognisable to me and I can never forgive her for the ordeal she put us through at Burcott House – or the incident with Sasha on the mountain edge.

I can't comprehend the things she did and I wish our lives had been different, but she was still my daughter. I just hope she is now at peace.

Ophelia sniffs and it snaps me out of my reflections. Hayley guides Ophelia to us and the four of us stand with our arms around each other at the graveside. Earth is thrown down onto Erin's wooden coffin and Ophelia tosses in a single red rose.

'Amen,' the vicar says.

It's over.

A single tear slides down my cheek and I wipe it away with a gloved hand. Today I have to be strong for Ophelia. I take a deep breath and square my shoulders.

We don't stay by the graveside long. There's no reason to linger. Hayley links arms with me and guides me to the waiting car. I let her take over, feeling suddenly exhausted. Lowering myself down onto the leather seat of the car, I hear the clicking of cameras. One persistent photographer seems to have snapped an image of me in my black outfit as I leave the most anticipated funeral of the year. I'm sure they've captured the photo they've been waiting for and that it will sell for a good price, given how prominent my family is in the news once more.

Out the corner of my eye, I see a police car slide into position behind us as we pull out of the church carpark. I'm thankful for the protection it represents but I still shield my face with one hand to make it harder for anyone else to take a picture of me in my most vulnerable moment, without my permission.

Andrew drives us back to my home and we all sit quietly, deep in our thoughts. On my request, he drives us past Burcott House on the way. This will be the last time I go anywhere near the place but I had to see it: the bright red 'For Sale' sign. Ophelia and Jasper both agreed they didn't want the house any more. It went on the market very quickly. It may take longer to sell because of recent events there and the damage done by the fire but the estate agent said it also might be snapped up sooner because of the infamous murders that have happened here. I guess it all depends on the buyer.

Ophelia is sitting by my side on the backseat of the car. She gazes out at the place that was her childhood home, the place where she'd planned her future to be. I've been watching her in case her grief becomes too much or in case the experience she's been through triggers any unusual behaviour. So far, she has been sad but she's also been composed and grown-up in her approach to what happened with her mother. The last thing I want is for this to push my granddaughter over the edge. I am going to keep a very close eye on her from now on.

As we drive down the winding country lane, it feels like this moment marks the end of an era for the Bailey family. I hope the next chapter and the future for my daughters and grandchildren will be much brighter. Leah seems to be happy with Tiana; I pray that Sasha and Douglas will get through his health issues together; and my darling grandchildren have the rest of their lives ahead of them. My wish is that they make better choices than the generations before them and I will do everything in my power to ensure they all have good relationships with each other.

I'm moving on too. After escaping the fire, it really hit home that life is too short. None of us know what's around the corner. So I've accepted the offer of a date with Gareth. I've spent too much of my life living in fear of Craig and grieving Simon. Gareth is a good man and I want to grab the chance of happiness in my golden years.

I can't do anything to change the past but I will do everything I can to protect my family and keep them safe, until my last breath.

Epilogue, Part Two
Lydia Knight

She's wearing the classic combination of a dark hat with a veil, a knee-length black dress and high-heeled shoes. She wobbles slightly as she lowers herself into the sleek, silver car and is whisked away from the graveyard and the eagle-eyed journalists who've been waiting hours to snap one photograph. A police car pulls out behind the vehicle she is in and my opportunity to follow Nadia Bailey is gone.

But there will be other days.

I'm prepared to wait until the right moment to confront her.

She's playing the part of the grieving mother, and she's playing it well. Except I discovered that she was estranged from her daughter Erin for years – I've heard all about their arguments and problems. And I know that her heartache could never, ever compare to mine.

I loved my son more than anything. We were as close as any mother and child could be. The day I got the call to tell me that my darling Xavier had been found dead in a ski chalet was the worst day of my life. He was always full of energy and had so much that he wanted to do. I still can't believe he's gone. Every morning feels like *Groundhog Day* when I wake up and remember that I'll never see him again. I'm living through a nightmare that no-one should have to experience.

Craig Turner was accused of his death. There was a horrible, drawn-out trial as the evidence was not concrete and the jury spent ages deciding on whether he was guilty but the man was eventually convicted to twenty-five years. It was not enough punishment for what he'd done but my solicitor assured me the sentencing would mean Craig would die behind bars. I was relieved that my son's killer had been put away. After the sentencing, I attempted to heal from the pain of losing Xavier. I tried everything – meditation, sleeping pills, alcohol, running, gratitude journals, moving house, reiki and the list goes on. Nothing worked. I spiralled becoming more and more desperate to find peace.

Then, only a few years later, Craig escaped from prison. There were reports of him being abroad in sun-drenched locations but he never came close to being caught. I seethed and raged at the injustice of my son's killer being free when my boy was dead. But I also found a purpose. I directed all of my thoughts and energy into playing detective, trying to work out where Craig was. I even flew out to some of the locations where he'd supposedly been seen. My quest to find him consumed me.

It's only been recently, as I've unravelled more about Craig and his life, that I've started to put the pieces of what really happened to Xavier together. I had plenty of doubts about whether Craig really did kill my darling son but I made myself believe that the judge and jury had got the conviction correct. It's taken me all of this time to unpick the misinformation and the lies. It became clear to me that Craig, despite his previous record for murder, was not the person who took my son's life.

I started to wonder more and more about the Bailey family and their connection with Xavier. All my questions circled back to one woman, Nadia Bailey. There was a lot of speculation about the evidence she gave; it was her word against her ex-partner's in court. Was she telling the truth or did she lie? And if she did, why?

I was determined to discover who my son's murderer really was. I knew it couldn't change things and that it wouldn't bring Xavier back but I had a burning desire to find out the truth. It was the most important thing to me and the sole focus of my days. It drove my husband and I apart. It fractured most of my friendships as no-one could understand why I kept probing and why I couldn't let things go.

Almost ten years after Xavier's death, I know what happened to him. A woman called Marnie told me everything. My suspicions were correct.

It was Nadia Bailey. She killed my son.

She did it to protect her own daughters because Xavier had gotten too close to the Bailey sisters. He knew one of their darkest secrets. A secret that Nadia was prepared to kill for to try to keep it buried. Although less than twenty-four hours after Xavier died and Erin Bailey went missing. Something obviously went wrong in Nadia's carefully laid plans and Xavier's death just seems all the more senseless as a result.

Nadia pinned the murder on the man she hated most in the world: Craig Turner. Marnie has told me all of the back history she knows. She contacted me out of the blue. I've had countless hoax calls and disappointments so I put the phone down when she first rang me to say she had information about the night Xavier died. I blocked her number but Marnie was persistent and she kept ringing until finally I relented and listened to what she had to say. I was shocked.

It turns out Marnie knew the Baileys very well. Marnie had been a neighbour of Erin's at the French ski resort and she knew a lot about the family. She became a close friend of Erin's, and she stayed by her side in the years when Erin was living incognito and the rest of the world was still hooked on the story of her mysterious disappearance. I remember Marnie's eyes misting as she told me Erin was like the daughter she never had. She was reeling from the news of Erin's death and convinced that Nadia had something to do with it. This had been the prompt for her to get in touch with me.

Erin had told Marnie all about the Bailey family's fallings-out and feuds. During the fateful skiing trip, Marnie had been watching the family reunion with interest and she'd observed the comings and go-ings from the ski chalet.

On one occasion, she followed Nadia, who had gone over to Xavier's ski chalet, having apparently had minimal interaction with him previously. Marnie saw her exiting the chalet around the estimat-ed hour of his death and she even witnessed Nadia disposing of the outfit she'd been wearing. It could've been a coincidence of course, but Marnie spoke with Nadia the day after and it didn't take much to see she had something to hide. Then she overheard a conversation that Nadia had with her daughter Sasha that confirmed what she believed.

Everything Marnie told me made sense; I knew in my gut she was telling me the truth.

I'm not going to let Nadia get away with it. She's going home to a house full of family who will help her through the grief of her daughter's passing. She has grandchildren to put a smile on her face and help her forget her sadness. I will never know what it's like to see my son get married or to hold the next generation of children in my arms.

Nadia Bailey is finally going to pay for what she's done. And I can't wait to get my revenge. After all, everyone gets their comeuppance at some point and Nadia is long overdue hers...

If you loved *Her Daughter's Lies* you can order *The Secret Marriage*, the next twisty psychological thriller by bestselling author Mikayla Davids.

Get it here!

If you're a fan of festive thrillers then check out *The Christmas Holiday*, another chilling psychological thriller by Mikayla Davids. Or read on for an extract...

Extract: The Christmas Holiday

Prologue

Now

I trudge through the snow, my breath coming out in puffs, visible in front of me in the frosty air. I scan the hazy horizon, I can barely see anything past the end of my own outstretched hand.

My feet sink into the clean snow. There are no other footprints, no one else has been here for some time. So where is everybody? How have I managed to get so lost?

I keep walking, slow heavy steps, my boots are dragging me down and my body aches with the effort it takes to keep going. I can't stop, I need to get back to the lodge, otherwise I'll freeze to death out here.

The snow is coming down hard now and, just as I start to despair, I see a light in the distance. It must be the holiday lodge where I'm staying with my family. It has to be.

I stumble forward, eager to get inside, to find warmth. But then I see something in the snow, just ahead of me. Something still and unmoving on the ground. But it's unmistakeable.

A body.

Spread out like a snow angel, hair fanning out across the white, soft blanket beneath it. A trickle of bright red blood from mouth to cheek, frozen in a moment of time. It looks unnatural, someone has positioned the person in exactly this way to make a statement.

That's when I hear the sirens. The blue flashing lights come closer. And then the German shepherd Garda dogs rush towards me, followed by the shouts of men in uniform.

They speed closer, the gap between us narrowing by the second. I'm clearly the target, but, any minute now, they're also going to spot the lifeless shape on the ground in front of me.

They will find me.

And they will find the dead body.

The Christmas Holiday is available to read now!

Extract: The Couple On Holiday

MIKAYLA DAVIDS

Prologue

I feel content and peaceful. A calm settles over me. I can't imagine that anything bad could ever happen, here on this beautiful island...

This summer, I'm in paradise with my new husband by my side and my life couldn't be more perfect. Light is filtering through the trees as I fling my arms wide and finish my morning yoga routine. It's a ritual

I complete every day, stretching my body as the sun rises. I follow this by making a coffee and sipping the hot, sweet liquid as I go for a gentle stroll.

Each morning, I vary my walk, taking in a different scene on the private Caribbean island that's my home for the summer. Yesterday, I walked down to one of the beaches and allowed my toes to sink into the soft, inviting sand. I surveyed the clear blue sea and listened to the birds twittering in the treetops. Today, my feet take me in a completely different direction. I walk round the edges of the whitewashed villa that belongs to my family, and along the twisting path that leads to the high clifftop on the north side of the island.

I skirt along the edges of the clifftop, every so often daring myself to look at the vast drop below. As I move, the tension in my muscles loosens. I manage to cover a fair distance and I find myself nearing the section of the cliff which gives way to natural steps and leads down to an idyllic lagoon. It was the place me and my husband went to on the second night of our honeymoon, over a week ago. A smile plays across my lips as I remember our romantic evening together by the sea, under the stars.

Right now, the sky is awash with beautiful deep pinks, purples and oranges. The turquoise sea contrasts beautifully and it's like I'm looking at a painting. There's a slight breeze and I enjoy the feel of the wind rippling in my hair as I watch a small fishing boat bobbing in the water. I sigh deeply, embracing the day.

Straying to the top of the steps, I look down, wondering whether I have time to descend and take a dip in the ocean before my husband wakes up. But the thought goes straight from my mind as I gaze down the steep, stony staircase and see a red trail of blood.

I freeze, panicked by the sight. It's not just a few blood spots, there's a lot of dark, red blood.

Perhaps an animal has been hurt? Or maybe someone is in trouble?

I take a deep breath, not really wanting to look again but knowing I'd never forgive myself for turning away if I could help in some way.

I stand on the first step and look down at the dizzying drop below. My nails are digging hard into the palms of my hands. I can't see anything, so I take another step, and then another until I'm part way down the route to the lagoon.

And then I see it.

I see the body, crumpled at the foot of the steps. The neck at an unnatural angle.

No-one could survive a fall like that.

I turn around, wanting to put some distance between me and the dead person, knowing I need to report what I've seen straight away. Instead, I'm jolted by the figure now standing on the top step looking down at me.

My heart hammers in my chest and I fight to keep my balance and stay upright.

Am I next?

The Couple on Holiday is available to read now!

Extract: The Christmas Party

Prologue

I spin with my sister in the middle of the dance floor, our hands clasped tight, whirling round to the music just as we did when we were children. The DJ is playing yet another classic Christmas tune and we both shout along at the tops of our voices, smiles wide, eyes bright, mirroring each other. Rainbow-coloured disco lights shine across the vast room and the crowd around us shimmers and sparkles.

The moment I've been hoping for is finally here. After ten long years, my family are together under the same roof again. My two sisters, my mother, our children and our husbands. We're reunited after a decade of not speaking. But I don't want to think about the terrible night that shattered our family because I've waited for this day for a long time.

As the song ends, I stagger, wobbling on my high heels and putting a hand to my throbbing head. I feel a steadying arm loop through mine and I'm guided along the edges of the friends and family gathered here to celebrate in this exquisite hotel. The hotel that my wealthy husband and I own. We've spent the last five years remodelling the place and I've poured everything into making this building a beautiful home as well as a successful business. I've worked hard to be where I am today. I may have had a little help with my husband's money and contacts but I came from nothing. So tonight I'm proud to show off amongst my nearest and dearest. And I know I've earned every single one of the admiring looks that have come my way this evening.

Everyone else seems to be in the moment, lapping up the festive atmosphere, but I'm on edge and I can't seem to properly let my hair down, despite the champagne that's flowing. A huge Christmas tree dominates one corner of the room, while the warm gold and red colour scheme spills out across the rest of the space and throughout the multitude of plush rooms beyond. Everything looks perfect on the surface. But, right now, I need to get away from the party.

When I exit through the double doors, the noise instantly dims and I feel like I can breathe properly again. I make my way along a winding corridor, my sister's hand in mine, and then we swing open another set of double doors into the grand foyer. This is the dazzling focal point of the building, with its curved marble staircase and sweeping gallery complete with a glittering crystal chandelier.

The first thing I notice is the strange silence. The music from the party shut out by the soundproofing.

The second thing I notice is the dead body. Lying spread-eagled on the white marble floor, a pool of dark red blood surrounding the head like a halo.

I'm stunned, surely this can't be happening? But my sister inhales sharply next to me so I know I'm not imagining this.

This is not a horrible dream. It's real.

My heart is hammering in my chest and my mouth feels dry. I lift my chin and make myself look once more at the person lying on the floor. I immediately recognise the broken figure at the foot of the steep marble staircase.

And I scream...

The Christmas Party is **available to read now!**

Dear reader,

I hope you enjoyed reading *Her Daughter's Lies*. And, if you've read all three books in the series, I hope you were gripped by the third book featuring the Bailey family!

Thank you so much for choosing to read *Her Daughter's Lies*. If you want to receive a free short story, '*The Summer Vacation*', then you can sign up to my mailing list using the QR code or via the following link: https://subscribepage.io/MikaylaDavidsBooks to receive the story and hear all about my latest news and releases. (Your email address will never be shared and you can unsubscribe at any time.)

Subscribe!

The Christmas Party was the first novel I published. I wasn't ready to let go of the characters after just one book, so I then wrote *The Family Secret*, which took the Bailey family to the icy French Alps. As I was writing the second book featuring this complicated family, more secrets spun out and I very clearly saw in my imagination the final scenes of what has become the third book in the series. I knew I had to write it and take the story of the Bailey family one step further!

This trilogy, as my first, will always be very special to me. I've had lots of fun developing the Bailey family and their misdemeanours! I really hope that you've been entertained and enjoyed seeing the twists and turns across the three books. I may write another story following Lydia and her revenge at some point! For the moment, I wanted to tie up the various plot lines involving the Bailey family but keep the door open for a possible return. I personally love endings in the psychological thriller genre that leave you wondering what might happen next or completely turn everything you thought you knew on it's head. Unfortunately for the Bailey family, I just don't think they would go on to have a quiet life! So it intrigued me to think about what they might come up against in the future...

If you enjoyed the book, I would be hugely grateful if you could write a short review or add a star rating. Reviews are so important for authors and they really do help new readers to discover books.

Leave a review!

I love hearing from readers so please do feedback with reviews or you can contact me via social media.

All my thanks,

Mikayla Davids

Follow me on Twitter: @MikaylaDBooks

Follow me on Instagram: mikayladavidsbooks

Find me on Facebook: Mikayla Davids Books

Visit my website: www.MikaylaDavidsBooks.com

Acknowledgements

I want to say a huge thank you to my family and my friends for supporting me. I'd also like to thank everyone who's worked on this book with me. A big thanks to Charlotte and Rachel for their invaluable early insights and encouragement. Thank you to Rhian McKay for her excellent feedback and copyediting. Thank you to Natasha Hodgson for proofreading and final catches. To Bee's Bookshelf, thanks for such detailed editorial notes and for all of your on point comments, you make editing fun! To all my fabulous supporters in my VIP author group, I'm so grateful for you! Big thanks to the very kind and patient Kelly Lacey, and the incredible Love Books Tours team!

As an author, I've learnt a lot along the way while I've been writing these novels. Sitting here at my writing desk it feels like a big moment to say goodbye to the Bailey family. However, I'm so excited to continue on this writing journey – and there are more books coming, so watch this space!

Also by Mikayla Davids TPB

The Christmas Party: An absolutely addictive psychological thriller with a jaw dropping twist (The Bailey family psychological thrillers Book 1)

The Family Secret: A completely gripping psychological thriller full of incredible twists (The Bailey family psychological thrillers Book 2)

Her Daughter's Lies: An addictive and unputdownable psychological thriller with a killer twist (The Bailey family psychological thrillers book 3)

The Christmas Holiday: A totally gripping and addictive psychological thriller

The Couple on Holiday: A completely addictive and gripping psycho-logical thriller with a heart-stopping twist

ISBN: 978-1-917018-06-7

eBook ISBN: 978-1-917018-05-0

Printed in Dunstable, United Kingdom